GEMINI DIVIDED
BERYL TESO

To Mary,
With many thanks.
Without you, this book
— with all its faults —
would never have
been written

Beryl

Copyright © 2019 Beryl Teso
All rights reserved.
ISBN: 9781091381421

CONTENTS

Chapter 1 1
Chapter 2, Maggie 1949 8
Chapter 3, Rene 1951 14
Chapter 4, Rene 1954 19
Chapter 5, Maggie 1954 - 1957 22
Chapter 6, Helen 1956 - 1957 37
Chapter 7, Maggie 1957 41
Chapter 8, Rene 1957 49
Chapter 9, Maggie 1963 53
Chapter 10, Helen 1961 - 1963 56
Chapter 11, Maggie 1963 59
Chapter 12, Helen 1962 64
Chapter 13, Maggie 1963 68
Chapter 14, Helen 1965 72
Chapter 15, Maggie 1966 77
Chapter 16, Helen 1966 86
Chapter 17, Maggie 1967 90
Chapter 18, Helen 1966 94
Chapter 19, Maggie 1966 -1967 97
Chapter 20, Helen 1967 - 68 103
Chapter 21, Rene 1967 106
Chapter 22, Maggie 1967 109
Chapter 23, Rene 1968 114
Chapter 24, Helen 1968 118
Chapter 25, Maggie 1968 123
Chapter 26, Helen 1971 131
Chapter 27, Maggie 1971 137
Chapter 28, Helen 1971 144
Chapter 29, Maggie 1971 150
Chapter 30, Helen 1972 153
Chapter 31, Maggie 1971 156
Chapter 32, Helen 1971 165
Chapter 33, Maggie 1971 170
Chapter 34, Helen 1970 181

Chapter 35, Maggie 1971 187
Chapter 36, Helen 1971 190
Chapter 37, Maggie and Helen 1971 193
Chapter 38, Divorce 1977 – 1978 Maggie & Helen .. 201
Chapter 39, Maggie 1978 205
Chapter 40, Helen 1979 211
Chapter 41, Maggie 1980/81 214
Chapter 42, Helen 1981 227
Chapter 43, Maggie 1982 232
Chapter 44, Maggie 1982 / 83 242
Chapter 45, Helen and Maggie 1985 -1990 246
Chapter 46, Helen 1990 257
Chapter 47, Alex 1991 267
Chapter 48, Gerry & the Superintendent 1991 271
Chapter 49, Helen April 1991 281
Chapter 50, Mike Seymour and the DI 286
Epilogue, Helen 1995 292

ACKNOWLEDGMENTS

With many thanks to my friends Janet, Sandra, Pauline, Gladys, Vikki, Heather and Tony as without their help and encouragement, my first story with all its faults (I hope not too many), would never have been written. A very special thanks to Diny who steered me through all the technical stuff that is beyond me, needed to actually put into book form.

Chapter one

'What are they screeching about now? I'd better go and sort them out before they kill each other. I emerged from the kitchen to hear Maggie yelling down from the landing.

'Are you deaf? Why don't you open the bloody door?' She was shouting down to her twin Helen, who was standing by the front door, defiantly ignoring the persistent ringing and not making any attempt to let the visitor in.

'It's Sheila, she's your friend. You open it.' her twin yelled back.

'I'm upstairs and you're right by the front door you miserable bitch,' an enraged Maggie responded.

'Whatever next, for goodness sake stop swearing,' I called out shocked by my daughter's language, and I opened the door myself to stop the racket. Sheila stood outside looking worried.

'Come on in Sheila love, Maggie's upstairs' I told her.

Why was it always like this? Why do my girls hate each other so much? Twins are supposed to have a special bond and love each other, especially identical ones, aren't they? Well something went wrong with my pair, because it's always been like this from the day they were born.

I decided to grab five minutes to have a cup of tea and a fag, and then I really will have to start preparing food for everyone. This animosity is exhausting and I feel I deserve a little break. They're nine years old now, and you really would think they would have grown out of this constant bickering. '

'Are you staying for tea Sheila? You are more than welcome' I called up the stairs.

'I'd love to if you don't mind Mrs Sutherland, thank you.' she responded.

'Course I don't mind.'

I worry about that girl. I wonder why she never wants to go home.

My husband Colin has been hiding in the shed again. He pretends he hasn't heard them rowing, that way he doesn't have to deal with the problem. He never wants to be the bad guy, and leaves that role to me. I love him to bits though, and I am very lucky to him as my husband.

'Any chance of a cuppa?' He called out from the shed.

'The kettle has just boiled, so come and join me luv'. I shouted back. We sat down together in the kitchen, and I don't know why but I found myself in a very reflective mood.

'Do you remember when the twins were born?' I asked him.

'Yeah, course I do. It was 10th June 1938 in the London Hospital just before the war, and Maggie didn't leave there for weeks because she was so small and you had to visit her every day,' he snapped at me. How could I forget?

'I was a twin you know. She was called Collette'.

'Rene,' he sounded irritated, 'you've told me that a thousand times over the years.'

I carried on, ignoring his complaint. I know I annoy him sometimes when I go on about things that can't be changed, but sometimes I feel I need to speak about the past s whether he likes it or not.

'Colette died a month after she was born, and all through my life I have felt a void, as if something or someone was missing, which can only be explained by her loss. Mum told me twins are connected by a special bond, they're like two magnets that become an inseparable whole and ...' he interrupted me. I wish he wouldn't do that.

'Well our two obviously haven't read the Twins Behaviour Manual,' he said and beetled off back to the shed again. He makes these amazing galleons there out of balsa wood, with all the rigging and brass name plates. They are fantastic reproductions, but I won't have them in the house because with our son Rhys crashing about all over the place they would get smashed to bits in no time. Well that's the excuse I give Colin, but I don't like them because they are dust traps and I've got enough housework to do without worrying about them getting broken. He's got a whole fleet of them on the shelves in his shed. I feel really mean not letting them in the house because I'm very lucky to have him as a husband. He loves me, and I love him and he is very kind and a good father. Bugger, my tea has gone cold and my cigarette has gone out, but I'm still reluctant to start getting the tea. I don't enjoy cooking one little bit.

Later, when I was chopping vegetables for the evening meal, I found myself continuing to reminisce. Odd really, there had not been anything that had happened in the past few days that has triggered this trip down memory lane.

The girls were supposed. This may have been because of the difference in their birth weights. Helen was a beautiful baby, just over seven pounds, a satisfactory weight for any baby but a really good weight for a twin. She was all pink and chubby, I couldn't stop cuddling her and I bonded with her from the minute I set eyes on her. But Maggie was a poor little scrap and only weighed in at three pounds. I was told it was touch and go as to whether she would live, but she was always a fighter and made it against the odds. But to my shame I never really bonded with her the same way I did with her sister. It was difficult as she was such a scrawny little thing, and with all those wires coming out of her she didn't look like a baby at all. I wasn't able to cuddle her for weeks. Maggie is still shorter than Helen and definitely not as pretty, she's a bit podgy too and her hair looks very dull compared with Helens glossy mane. Maggie often yells at me 'you've always loved her more than me' and the guilt sweeps over me, because it's true.

I can hear Rhys moving about. You can **always** hear Rhys moving about as he seems incapable of doing it quietly. Here he comes, crashing down the stairs two at a time obviously in search of food. You'd think I never feed him the amount he gobbles down every meal time. He was a little present Colin left for me after his first leave from the army. He was called up early because he belonged to a Territorial Army group or brigade; I never knew what they called it. Rhys is seven now, born in December 1940 Not the best of times to have a baby as the Blitz was raging from September of that year, and didn't stop until the following May. We were lucky in this part of London as we didn't have a lot of bomb damage, nevertheless we had to sleep in the Anderson shelter every night and endure the terrifying sounds of bombs and gunfire. Try that with a small baby and a pair of two year olds fighting a war all of their own in a confined space. When we emerged in the mornings the sky was red on the horizon from all the fires burning in the docks and East End of the city. Bloody terrifying it was.'

'Mum I'm starving.'

I was awakened from my reverie by Rhys's **very** loud voice.

'So what's new?' I laughed. 'Come and give me a cuddle, then go back upstairs and I'll give you a shout when it's ready.'

Chapter two
Maggie 1949

I made sure I failed the eleven plus, and thank goodness I did. There was no way I wanted to go to that stuck up grammar school with darling Helen. Mum was told she would pass the eleven plus easily, but I was not mentioned. Who am I kidding? I would have failed anyway without any extra effort on my part. I have had Helen shoved in my face all through my school years, and by going to a different school I wouldn't have to endure that anymore. Whoopee!

You're not like you sister are you? She does as she's told. Where's your homework? Helen would have done hers on time,' and on and on in the same vein all through until now as I am due to start my new school today without Helen. I can't help feeling nervous, but excited at the same time.

My last teacher, Mrs Jones, told me it would be the right one for me and I would love it. She had always helped me if I had trouble with any of my lessons, so I trust her opinion. I hope she's right. It used to be called a Central School, which was in between the grammar and the thicko's school, and Mrs Jones said they were experimenting with new forms of education because so many children had their schooling disrupted because of the war, and a new system would be required for the future that would be unlike any previous form of state education, The school I was going to had been selected as one of the ones to try out new systems, and it would be mixed boys and girls, not single sex like the grammar. Goodee! You don't get boys in there; they segregate them off into different schools. I like boys.

I told Mum I was nervous. .

'Silly girl, you'll be fine. It's Helen's first day too and she's not worried, and she's going to the Grammar.

Whatever made me think I would get any sympathy from Mum? She's on cloud nine that Helen is going to that bloody school; you would think she had been sanctified. Mum's boring all her friends and family to death, also people she had never met before that we pass in the street. *Did you know my daughter Helen's going to the grammar*? I don't know why she doesn't get one of those loud hailer things they use at Rhys's football ground to make doubly sure **everybody** in the district knows. It would be nice if just for once she would realise that I'm NOT Helen, I'm ME. Maybe it's because we are twins she thinks we should be the same in every way. I don't think she will ever stop comparing us, and I will always come out as the underdog.

Looking back, I needn't have worried about starting the new school, I loved it from day one, and more to the point, it seemed to love me. The teachers were great and very encouraging, and I've made a lot of friends. Sheila is in the same class as me which is fantastic.

Maggie 1952

I couldn't wait to tell Mum and Dad where we had been today.

'You will never believe what we did at school today?' I gabbled. 'We went to visit an archaeological dig and we were allowed to help out a bit.'

'Well they might have let the parents know you would be wallowing in the mud, and then you could have worn different clothes instead of getting your uniform dirty'.

Typical Mum! She's only ever worries about how clean our clothes are, and thinks she will be judged by that. Who's going to judge her I cannot imagine. Maybe God's got a big register up there in heaven and lists one of Mrs Rene Sutherland's misdemeanours, that her daughter had mud on her clothes in 1952. One of her other worries is supposing we got knocked over by a bus, what the doctors would think your Mother was like if you had a dirty gym slip? I somehow think they might be more interested in whether I was dead or not rather than the state of my clothes. I tried to grab her interest again.

'The site was closed down at the beginning of the war and has only just been reopened again. They want volunteers to help this week-end. Please can I go Mum?' Helen had to stick her nose in naturally.

'What's so exciting about grovelling about in the mud' she said. That's not going to get through your exams. I've been translating Virgil today, much more interesting.' she said, and flounced out banging the door after her. Poor old Dad, he always has to fix the doors, because one of us has banged them too hard as we sweep out of the room, trying to make our point. I don't think she enjoyed translating that bloke, whoever he is one little bit. Good!

Two of the boys in our commercial class wanted to be journalists and asked Mr Hewitt if we could have a photography class as they thought it would help them to get a job He said he would arrange it. I wouldn't mind being a journalist. When I mentioned it to Mum, Helen, in her usual obnoxious way, said my English wasn't good enough for that. Bitch! Do you know, I think she might be a teeny bit jealous of me? Anyway Mum said I could go. I guess she sees it as one way of getting me out of the house.

Chapter three
Rene 1951

Not before time Colin decided to clear out all the rubbish in his shed, which I don't think he has done since before the war. He is all excited about an old picnic basket he has unearthed that his parents used when they took him and his brother out on day trips.

'Our kids have missed out on the family outings because of the war, so why don't we all go on a coach trip to Brighton?' he said all excited at the idea.

I had a sense of foreboding at the thought of our three going out together. – that's not fair -- I should have said two, as Rhys was rarely any trouble, but just to be bloody minded the girls will argue as to where we should or shouldn't go, each of them wanting to do something different, but I didn't say anything as I don't want to spoil it for Colin. He seems so thrilled at the idea.

'Fancy going down to Brighton for the day kids?' he enthused. They stared at him looking mystified.

'What for?' Rhys piped up.

'For enjoyment' he replied, it'll be fun

'I have to write an important essay this weekend' Helen interrupted.

'For goodness sake surely you can do that on Sunday?' Colin challenged her. She sniffed, but didn't argue, thank goodness.

'Great idea Dad, I've never been to Brighton' Maggie said.

'Course you haven't stupid, and as the rest of us haven't been, it's obvious you haven't either.' Helen interjected.

Here we go I thought, this trip does not bode well.

Colin booked the coach, I packed sandwiches, chocolate biscuits, thermos flasks, and anything else I could find into the picnic basket and off we went. The weather was fine, so at least that's one less complaint we will have to endure.

'What's in Brighton then?' Rhys piped up.

'There used to be waxworks museum there before the war. I don't know if it is still there as it may have been bombed. That was always fun to go around.' They all looked him Colin blankly.

'What else is there?' Maggie asked.

'It's a nice day so we can go down to the beach and paddle in the sea.'

'Ooh goodie goodie!'

'Whatever for?' piped up Helen. I was waiting for her to come up with some sort of objection. Proud of her though I am, she really has become the most frightful snob since she went to that school. However Maggie has flourished in hers. I would love to have done the things she does there. All our teachers did was make sure we knew enough to get through our school leaving certificate at fourteen, which only qualified the boys for crappy jobs in factories, London Transport, or as meter readers for the Gas Board, which is what Colin does for a living, and the girls to be shop girls or skivvies.

Colin and I sat in separate seats so we could split the girls up to stop arguments and prevent them showing us up. Rhys had to sit next to a very fat lady which didn't please him. She kept talking to him – not that she ever got a reply, but she looked happy enough just to have someone to address her remarks to, probably lonely poor old dear. When we arrived in Brighton the sun was blazing away in a cloudless sky, and there were banners across the roads announcing a carnival.

'Fantastic, I think there is some sort of festival going on. That'll be fun wont it? Colin said.

'Why?' Rhys said. How do you answer that? Colin and I looked at each other and didn't bother to reply. It started to go downhill soon after that. When Helen realised there was a museum in the town, she insisted we went to visit it.

'Dad there's a fair on the Pier, can we go there?' Maggie requested.

'Yeah let's,' Rhys agreed, but naturally Helen objected and insisted we should go to the museum. That caused a shouting match to break out. A cloud crossed Colin's face which upset me as he had been looking so happy from the moment we got on the coach. It ended up with me taking Helen to the museum, something I really didn't want to do, and Colin taking the other two down to the beach, which I would have enjoyed.

'The museum was most interesting; much better than messing about in the sea.' Helen said in her grammar school voice. I really don't know who she thinks she is these days. Maggie turned on her.

'Splashing about in the sea is what you come to the seaside for you snobby cow. We can go to the museums in London any time. Did you enjoy it Mum?'

'Not much dear, but please don't call your sister names' I replied. Helen sniffed, but fortunately didn't say anything. Not quite the outing Colin had planned.. We all met up again for our picnic later on, but the girls kept sniping at each other, so once again we split the family up for the rest of the day. We didn't see the Carnival, as the kids didn't seem to be interested in the idea. Nobody spoke on the coach going home, and I resolved never to attempt going out as a family again. It was far too exhausting.

Chapter four
Rene 1954

I can't believe it, the girls are sixteen. Where did all those years go? Decisions need to be made about their future. Helen announced she wanted to go on to university.

'Do ordinary people like us go to university?' I asked Colin. 'I thought University was only for 'posh' people with money, not working class kids like Helen.' He looked a bit worried but didn't say anything. I'm really worried as I don't see how we can afford for her to go. There will be all those books to pay for and heaven knows what else. Maggie has stayed on at her school for another year to improve her English because she wants to be a journalist. Did you ever! I'm sure she's not clever enough to do job like that. Colin says I underestimate her. She could have left last year when she was fifteen and get a job which I wanted her to do. Her class teacher Mr Hewitt thought she was quite capable of following her choice of career, and he took her to meet his friend Jim, who was the editor of The Echo, our local rag, and he agreed to take her on as an apprentice if she stayed on at school to get an O level in English. She did that and passed, and now she is going to start work on the paper next month. Maybe she's cleverer than I think she is?

Colin said we must go to see Miss Harrison, Helen's Head Mistress, and ask her if there are any grants available to help with expenses if she goes to university. She is one of the most terrifying females I have ever met, and there is no way I would dare ask her anything. Colin's made of sterner stuff than me and he made an appointment for Wednesday the following week and insists I go with him.

It's Wednesday the day I was dreading. Colin knocked on Miss Harrison's door.

'Do come in Mr and Mrs Sutherland. I'm expecting you' she boomed. I wondered if it was part of the training course to teach head teachers to roar like sergeant majors in order to intimidate errant children and timid parents? Feeling about five years old we entered he office. Colin started to talk to her.

'I would be very grateful for any ...'

'Speak up Mr Sutherland, I can't hear you' she bellowed.

I wanted to leave there and then, but bless my Colin's heart, he started again.

'My wife and I are worried that our daughter Helen wants to go to university.'

'Worried man? Whatever for?' she barked. 'Surely you must be delighted?'

'Yes we are but we are not well off and are wondering if there are any grants available that can help people like us?' He managed to blurt out before she interrupted him again. I was so proud of him.

'Of course there are. There are several ... This time asserting himself Colin cut Miss Harrison off mid-stream in case she launched herself into a long tirade that he didn't understand.

'How can I access this help is what we want to know?' he said to her.

We left her office armed to the teeth with forms for available grants and found it wasn't going to cost us a penny. Isn't that amazing?

Chapter five
Maggie 1954 - 1957

I absolutely love my job and I am learning as much as I can from the older, more experienced journalists on the paper. Mathew Prentice is my main source of information and he is a real sweetie, and I wondered what a gifted man like him was doing working on a local paper, so one day I asked him if he had ever wanted to work for one of the Nationals. There was a long pause before he answered me, and I realised it was cheeky — no, actually downright rude of a girl of my age asking such a personal question to a much older man. I could feel myself blushing.

'Beware the demon drink he warned me. It's the downfall of many a good journalist. Once upon a time I worked in Fleet Street for most of the Nationals. I rose up the ladder and progressed from dogsbody to gossip columnist, then to foreign correspondent, and eventually editor until the drink got me and I became a hopeless unreliable drunk, and lost my job. The tragedy is I haven't touched a drop in years, but once a drunk, always a drunk as far as Fleet Street is concerned and even when I'd kicked the habit, nobody would employ me. I knew Jim, our editor, when I was at the height of my career, and he rescued me by giving me a job here on the ECHO, for which I will be forever in his debt.

'Thank you for telling me .I didn't mean to pry, I'm sorry.'

'Just remember my warning when you move on from here. Now we can go to the pub and you can buy me a drink. Mines a lemonade' he said.

Sheila's family had moved to Paddington and we missed each other, so we tried to meet up in town regularly. One week we were having such a good time dancing at the Lyceum that I didn't notice the time and missed my last train. 'Never mind' Sheila said 'come and stay with me' not sounding very enthusiastic though which surprised me as she had stayed at my house countless times, and mum was always feeding her.

Then I found out why she was so reluctant to return the hospitality. As she opened the front door we were greeted with shouting then a shriek of terror and the sight of Sheila's mother lying on the floor with blood streaming from her head with Sheila's father standing over her, his arms raised ready to beat her again.

'Get off of her you bastard' Sheila screamed as she rushed over to help her sobbing mother to her feet. I was struck dumb with horror. I simply couldn't believe what I had witnessed. I thought of my mild mannered parents who would never hit each other, and the only raised voices in our house were Helen's and mine, but even then we never resorted to hitting each other. Then her father raised his fist again, this time to strike Sheila when he spotted me.

'Who's that tart you have brought into MY house?' he yelled. Sheila ignored him so he stormed out of the house slamming the door behind him.

'Sorry you had to witness that Mag's. Give me a hand to get mum upstairs to bed will you'. Later she told me it had always been like that in her house which was why she had never taken me home with her before. The whole episode really upset me and I would like to have spoken to my Dad about it, but if Helen saw me having a serious conversation with him, she would but in. I suppose I would do the same if I thought she was being favoured. Why do we hate each other so much? It's pathetic really.

At work the following day I kept thinking about Sheila's dad.

'You're unusually quiet girlie, everything OK?' Mathew asked me.

'I'm fine' I said at first, and then I told him what I had witnessed at Sheila's house that week-end.

'Very common I regret to tell you' he said. I didn't believe him and it must have shown in my face.

'Unfortunately these violent blokes often get away with just a warning, basically because nobody in authority actually believes this sort of thing goes on, or may even think the woman asked for it.'.

'Surely not' I questioned him. 'Does that mean Sheila's mum hasn't got a leg to stand on as far as the law is concerned?'

'That's about it' Mathew replied. 'If the woman leaves her husband, she wouldn't have anywhere to go unless she had a supportive family, but if she didn't have, she would find herself homeless. Also, by leaving the family home she would lose any claim to it, which is another reason many of these women stay with their abusive husbands.'

'That's shocking' I said, 'I can't believe that could happen in this country'.

'You want to be a proper journalist don't you? Well go and do some research on domestic violence and write an article about it. You never know it could just change things. Look up old court cases in newspapers – you will find those in the library. Go and see Alison Cartwright, she's a family lawyer and an old friend of mine, and she will tell you stories that will make your hair stand on end. I'll help you put the whole thing together, but you will have to do the research yourself.' Research? Write and research a whole article? God was I ready for that?

'How do I begin?' I asked him. Silly question I realised as soon as I said it.

'Get your arse off that chair for starters and tell Jim where you're going and why, and then get on with it.'

I was shaking like a leaf when I went to see our editor, hoping he would say no, I couldn't go, but he OK'd the idea, so quaking I set off for the library to read up all I could find on the subject.

'Where would I find Alison?' I asked Mathew and I knew immediately I had made another mistake as he gave me a look that could kill.

'Don't keep asking me what to do. You're supposed to be a journalist, aren't you? Well get on with it and don't keep bothering me every five minutes.'

I felt like crying. He had always been so kind, and now he was yelling at me. I looked in the telephone book under solicitors and there she was, Alison Cartwright & Associates at an address in the High Street. Now I had to phone and make an appointment to see her.

'May I speak to Alison Cartwright please? Mathew Prentice suggested I should ring her for advice.' I gabbled to the receptionist nervously.

'I'll see if she's available' she answered in that snooty why she would want to speak to you kind of voice that receptionists use. That didn't help my nerves one little bit.—Maybe I'm not good enough to be a journalist I thought – then a picture of Mum and Helen sneering at me popped into my mind saying, 'we told you wouldn't be able to do that job,' and I pulled myself together. I'll show 'em I can I told myself.

Alison was lovely. She spoke to me in such a kind way my nervousness vanished immediately.

'Mathew and I have been friends from the time when he worked for the COURIER and I worked in Lincolns Inn.' she told me, and said that he had telephoned her to expect my call. Bless him. He wasn't being horrible; he just wanted me to think for myself.

'Meet me for lunch tomorrow' she said 'One-o-clock at JULES. Bye.'

Lunch in a posh restaurant? Wow, but I haven't got enough money for a place like that, and I've never been to a smart restaurant before – actually I haven't been in ANY restaurant before, apart from cheese on toast in Joe Lyons once. How will I know which knife and fork to use? Panic set in. I felt very young and gauche, and didn't know about expense accounts and just how much business was conducted in pubs and restaurants then. I've made up for it since, but that comes later.

Alison was brilliant and ordered for the both of us so I didn't have to plough through the menu which was not only enormous, but in French. As we had the same meal I watched her to see what cutlery she used, so that was no problem and I started to enjoy myself – that was until she started to tell me stories of some of the domestic abuse cases she had handled. I was near to tears; I simply couldn't believe that men could treat their wives and children, who they were supposed to love and care for so cruelly.

'All sorts of reasons' she told me. 'Jealousy, feelings of inadequacy: sometimes it was because it had happened to them when they were kids, and they thought it was normal for men to treat their wives that way'. Then she told me about a friend of hers called Molly she had met at a local book club.

'I'd known her for about a year before I asked her about her husband. 'Oh' she said cheerfully 'He's dead; killed in a freak road accident'. I was surprised she seemed pleased about it and it must have shown on my face. She told me he was a total bastard and knocked her and their kids and about, and he had completely demoralised her and taken away all her confidence, so she didn't have the courage to leave him. That was five years ago and she is fine now, and once a week she runs a small group for women who have had similar experiences, and they offer support to each other.

I'll give her a ring and see if she will meet you. Would you like that?'

'Alison that would be fantastic. Thank you so much.' I suddenly thought I can do this and looked forward to meeting Molly.

I arranged to meet Molly at her at her house after she had dropped her children off at school.

'It's very kind of you to see me.' I told her as I was trying not to stare at the scars on her arms the vicious red line around her neck as if someone had tried to strangle her. 'This is my first solo assignment.' I continued.

A cloud passed over Molly's face, and I realised that was the wrong thing to say , so I told her how I had seen my friend Sheila's father beat her mother up in front of me, and I couldn't believe anyone could do that to someone they are supposed to love, which is why I am researching the subject now.' Her expression changed.

'Just for a minute I thought you were just being a nosey journalist out for a sensational story,' she explained.' Phew! I nearly blew it there. I must learn to phrase my questions more carefully.

She told me that her husband had been kind gentle and loving until their first child was born.

'I don't know if it was jealousy that made Sean turn. Soon after Susie was born, he was watching me bath her and I stupidly thought he was admiring his first born, but when I asked him to pass me a towel he hit me round the head knocking me on the floor swearing at me at the same time. He was using disgusting words that I had never heard before. Later he was full of apologies telling me he didn't know what came over him and that it would never happen again. I learned later that this was standard with these violent men and they fooled many a girl into believing them -- as I did then. However, it happened again the following week, and the day after that, and I endured constant beatings from the bastard over the five years of our marriage, until I became a pathetic wimp always trying to please this monster in order to avoid punishment. When I became pregnant again the beatings became a daily occurrence. It's amazing I went full term with little Bob.'

'Did you try to get help from your doctor?' I asked her.

'Fat lot of good he was. He had been Sean's family doctor when he was a lad, and said I should make allowances for him because he had endured a terrible childhood, and asked me if I had provoked him?'

The fact he was creating a terrible childhood for his own kids didn't seem to occur to the idiot. I suppose. I should have changed doctors immediately, but I had become so unsure of myself by this time I seemed to be incapable of making a decision by myself. Men like Sean do that to you.'

'I'm not surprised' I interjected. What about your mum?'

'There was no bloody help coming from that quarter either. My mum accused me of being a bad wife and said he had hit me, to bring me into line can you believe?'

'And the police, what did they have to say? You did report him I take it?'

'Oh they just said they didn't interfere with domestics as they called them.'

I couldn't believe there was no help available for women in Molly and Sheila's mum's position. Mathew was right. I was horrified and getting angrier by the minute.

'Wasn't there **any** help available for you at all like the council or social services?'

'No, absolutely nothing. There has been a slight improvement since as this was five years ago, but it is still nothing like enough.'

She continued, telling me how he started to terrorise the kids and they were so frightened of him they didn't dare scream or cry when he hit them.

Her story got worse as he took to locking her up in the box room, where he had blacked out the windows and soundproofed the room so nobody could hear her shout and scream. He had lost his job by this time, so he took the kids to school himself, telling them Mummy was not well and couldn't take them anymore. He threatened all kinds of punishments if they ever told anyone he had hit them, and said he was doing it for their own good as they were possessed by the devil, and that's why he hit them, to beat the devil out.

'Can you imagine how terrified they were being told something like that?' Molly challenged me. I was close to tears by this time.

'The day he was killed the police came round to tell me about the accident he was involved in. Evidently a car had veered off the road to avoid a jay walker and crushed Sean against the wall killing him outright. My neighbour told them I was definitely in the house, so when I didn't answer the door they broke it down, and discovered me in the locked bed room. They looked a bit mystified but didn't ask me why I was in there. Then they told me what had happened to my husband and I burst into tears of joy at the news. The police thought they were tears of sorrow, but I enlightened them. Who do you think locks me in this room every day?' I yelled at them.

'You should have reported him to us ma'am,' the sergeant said.

'I did, and was told that he police didn't deal with domestics.. The copper did have the good grace to look sheepish when I told him of my experience with his lot. I was on a roll now, telling him this was the sort of thing that happens to women when you, dismiss their claims. Men like Sean get away with all manner of cruelty to their wives, and I wonder just how many are actually killed by them just because you -- the so called upholders of law and order -- won't help the women, and the men know it.' she said. I couldn't thank Molly enough for telling me her story.

'Obviously I won't use your name in my article but would you allow me to quote your story? 'I asked her.

'Yes but I would like you to show it to me first as I need to make sure there is nothing in it to identify either me or my children. I moved here to get away from the place where I had been so unhappy and I would hate any of my new friends at the school to know how my life used to be. They would think I was a pathetic female to let such things happen, not understanding how men like Sean can get under your skin and make you feel so feeble and helpless that you begin to think you deserve to be treated in that way.'

I asked Molly if she would introduce me to other women in her group who had suffered similar treatment from their husbands. She hesitated at first, but then said she would ask them at that afternoon's meeting, and, bless them; they agreed to tell me provided I didn't print their names. Meeting them gave me more information to call on for my article.

I pieced together court cases I had researched from newspapers in the library, Molly's story, and information I had gleaned from the group and I couldn't wait to get it all down. I ran over to a typewriter in the newsroom and bashed it out there and then

'OK girlie?' Mathew asked.' Need any help?'

'Not just yet' I told him, 'let me just get it all down first. He gave me a sideways glance, obviously expecting me to ask for him to help me, but I didn't at that stage, the story was writing itself. I think I gave him a big surprise when I handed the completed article to him.

'You've done well Maggie, really well. I'm proud of you. Give it to Jim'

'Don't you want to rewrite some of it?'

'No luv; it's raw and I think it would be wrong to mess with it.'

I was touched and felt the tears gathering. I wiped them away quickly. 'Didn't want Mathew to see me blub.

Chapter six
Helen 1956 - 1957

I was doing my homework when Maggie burst in the back door, calling out to Mum saying 'you'll never guess?'

'What's so important that you can't even say hello to your sister?' Mum questioned. She never stops trying to make us love each other.

'Sorry Mum, Hi Helen' Maggie gabbled. 'I'm no longer an apprentice at the paper.'

She was obviously waiting for Mum and me to ask her why.

'Have you got the sack then? I always said you wouldn't be able to hack it.' I asked her, rather nastily. I don't seem able to stop myself snipping at her.

'Far from it, the editor has ended my apprenticeship early and made me up to a full reporter on the strength of my article on domestic violence' she gabbled. 'He's hardly altered any of my script as he doesn't want to spoil the spontaneity of my writing he said. It's in tomorrow's edition. I'm getting a rise in my salary, and will be working with the big boys from now on. The Editor asked me if I had any ideas of my own on what the paper needed, and I don't think he thought I would come up with anything, but I told him it needs a regular column for young people – like me. He said he would think about it. Isn't that amazing?' she said with her eyes

I was seething. How did she manage to get that position so quickly? She's not that intelligent or ambitious. We're only seventeen, and I am still studying and stony broke, and I've got another four years in front of me before I earn a penny, and she's getting big money already. I'm supposed to be the high achiever not her. Never mind, my turn will come. Dad had walked in as she was gabbling on, and he gave her a huge hug.

'That's a real achievement isn't it Rene? You should congratulate her at best, and at least, give her a hug and a kiss he prompted Mum; and it wouldn't hurt you to compliment her on her promotion either Miss.' he said to me. Not having a lot of choice I did so without any enthusiasm. The next day Maggie's article came out and I would love to say it wasn't much good, but it was. It was full of compassion for these abused women, and indignation that there was nowhere they could seek help. Where did she learn to write like that? I expect the editor changed her report, but he still gave her the by-line.

There was a note from the Editor at the end of the report saying this situation was a total disgrace and the ECHO was going to run a petition to demand the government, the police and the local authorities to change their attitude and face the fact that violence against women was something nobody ever talked about, and yet it was commonplace in **all** walks of society. These women were being abused and beaten, and he wondered how many had actually died because there was **no** help available for them? The ECHO wanted to 'right this wrong', and he called upon the readers to add their name to the paper's campaign by signing their petition to alert the authorities that **something must be done to help these victims of appalling abuse.** I must say I was reluctantly impressed, and will definitely sign the petition, although I won't tell Maggie. Mum's comment was that she didn't really believe that sort of thing happened as much as Maggie had implied. She looked crestfallen then shrugged her shoulders. She couldn't win with mum as I was always her favourite, much to Maggie's chagrin.

Maybe I will congratulate her?

Nah!, Better not break the habit of a lifetime. Thank goodness, my exams are finished at last, and I think I will pass with four As. Now I'm in search of the best university I can find to complete my studies, and have made appointments at three of them for next week.

Chapter seven
Maggie 1957

I've been headhunted by the COURIER, a popular National paper with an enormous circulation, on the strength of my column for young people in the ECHO. I couldn't believe it, I'm only nineteen and they have offered me a whacking great salary increase to start with, and a promise of more in six months. I was very sad leaving the ECHO as I had been very happy there and everybody had helped me to become a journalist good enough to be approached by a national paper. They must have liked me as the staff clubbed together to buy me an expensive typewriter as a going away present. I burst into tears when Jim presented it to me. I always seem to be bursting into tears. I really must learn to keep my emotions at bay.

'Keep in touch girlie' Mathew said and I swore that I would.

'No you won't, not once you hit Fleet Street. I've seen it so many times before Mags. Good luck' he said and turned his back on me returning to his report as he said it. Was there a tear in his eye? I couldn't be sure.

I needed to move to a more central part of London for easier access to my job and Sheila agreed to share a room with me although her work place was not too far from her family home.

'What about your Mum?' I asked her thinking she wouldn't want to leave her alone with her brutal father, but as luck would have it, her brother Kevin, a six foot plus regimental boxer, had moved back into the family home after finishing his National Service, and he would make sure his father behaved himself. We found a bedsitting room in South Kensington which would do for starters.

The day I was due to start at the COURIER loomed. I was nervous but confident, as THEY had asked ME to work there, I hadn't had to grovel for the job. However, I was soon cut down to size. I was taken to the Personnel Department where a snooty woman whose hair seemed to be in competition with the Empire State building, peered over her glasses at me demanding to know who I was.

'I'm Maggie Suther. . . '

'Oh yeah, follow me' she commanded. She swept through the corridors of the enormous building, into the newsroom, dumped me on to the women's editor, and left abruptly.

'Who the hell are you?' this bad tempered looking woman demanded of me, looking down her nose as she said it. 'What's yer name?

'Maggie Sutherland, I'm from ...

'Oh yeah, I know who you are – or were. Here you are the lowest of the low. A mere child and a female one at that and you will learn that around these parts that don't count for much until you've proved yourself. Capiche?' What on earth did that mean?

'Call me Liz and get me a cup of coffee' she barked then turned her back on me and started to talk to a colleague. What happened to PLEASE and where do I get the coffee from? I felt like walking out of the door and returning to the ECHO where people spoke to you nicely, but of course I didn't. Maybe this was an initiative test she had set me? I saw a coffee machine where a young lad was standing who looked as bemused as I was.

'You lost luv? I bet Attila over there has ordered you to get her a coffee' He said. 'I was working in her department last week so I know how she likes it. She will bawl you out if it's wrong. I think I'm the male equivalent of you. We may have been rising stars on our local papers, but we are only the gofers round here. My name's Graham, known as Gray or Boy mostly. I hope that's going to change soon' he said.

My hand was shaking when I handed the coffee to Liz so I managed to spill some which engendered a curse from her, but when she tasted it she gave me a funny look but didn't complain. Thanks Graham, I owe you.

After a couple of days I got used to the banter, the teasing, the noise and the way everything was carried out at full speed. After a few weeks of starting there, a big story hit the news desks. A revolution had erupted in Hungary. It began as a student demonstration against the restrictive Russian communist regime and it quickly spread throughout the country. The Soviets initially agreed to negotiate terms with the revolutionaries to form a new democratically elected government, but then changed their minds; instead they sent tanks and troops to crush the rebels. Thousands were killed and two hundred thousand of them fled the country, with huge numbers of them arriving in London. The journalists were running in and out of the office in a state of excitement. I soon learnt that this was the norm when a big story broke. Then one of the sub editors called Liz to cover the human side of the refugees' story.

'Take the child with you and see if she can come up with a decent story.' The sub instructed her. Was I the child? Bloody cheek! Liz didn't look best pleased at the idea of me trailing after her on such an important assignment and showed it. I was thrilled and decided I would ignore her attitude and enjoy my first chance of covering a story of this magnitude. This quickly changed to a feeling of helplessness when I arrived at the holding centre where hundreds of mostly young refugees were crammed together in a hall that wasn't really big enough for so many people. There were lots of volunteers and officials handing out leaflets in Hungarian, saying what help was available from the local council offices once they had found somewhere to live, and also the availability of English lessons. The Women's Royal Voluntary Service (WRVS) were dolling out tea and biscuits along with kind words. There had been no time for them to pack anything when they fled, so all they possessed were the clothes they were wearing when they crossed the border. The women and children were either crying or looking traumatised, and the men -- or boys --, as they looked about my age, were trying to look as if they were in control of the situation. My heart went out to them.

'Try and get some sob stories out of them,' Liz instructed me quite coldly. Heartless bitch I thought. There was a pretty young woman with a baby close by so I spoke to her.

'What's your name I asked?' she glared at me. 'Do you speak English I continued?'

'Of course. Do you speak Hungarian?' she answered in a hostile voice.

'No, I think there are some translators . . .'

I realised I had made a big mistake and needed to start again with this poor girl.

'Sorry, I've offended you haven't I? I didn't mean to but this is my first big assignment for my paper and I'm still learning my job. Forgive me. I was hoping you would be kind enough to tell me about the ordeal you have suffered leaving your country. It must have been traumatic for you.' She softened.

'My name is Magda and my husband Jan taught at the university in Budapest. That was where the revolution started. Yesterday he burst into the kitchen, grabbed me and our baby and told me we have to leave NOW. I have another daughter who was at nursery school and I screamed at him what about Valeria? But he said there's no time, we must go **this minute.**' She started to cry and she was swaying to and fro. Her sobbing came from deep within her soul which of course set me off, and I had tears pouring down my face. Not very professional; I really am going to toughen up as I can't keep crying every time I hear a sad story.

'Will you be able to contact your mother to find out about Valeria?' I asked her.

'Of course not' Magda snapped. 'You people have no idea what life is like under the Soviets. I may never see or hear from my family ever again.' Her husband appeared and she started hitting him round the head with the sheaves of paper she had accumulated, and I recognised the name Valeria in the tirade she was subjecting him to.

I was making notes all the time and became totally absorbed with the variety of reasons these poor displaced people told me as to why they had fled their homes. They were now in fear of their lives, and knew if they stayed in Hungary they would be shown no mercy as all known revolutionaries would be shot. When we returned to the newsroom, Liz grumpily showed me how I should present my story to the sub editor. I think she wanted me to fail. Maybe I will have proved myself to her now as I had put my heart into my report. Nah! Probably not, but even though I say it myself, I think my words conveyed the suffering these displaced people had endured. I must have achieved this as the sub editor didn't alter a single word, nor did he congratulate me but I'm a fully blown reporter now, so he would expect me to turn out a decent report. I must remember that and not seek praise like a kid. One of the first things I did when I finally went home to our bed-sit was to check where Hungary was on the Atlas. I felt ashamed that I had no idea where it was, apart from the fact it was in Europe. God, I've got a lot to learn.

Chapter eight
Rene 1957

I had mixed feelings about the girls leaving home. I certainly don't miss the squabbling but I did worry about them eating properly. I wasn't too bothered about Helen as she would be living in halls she tells me and will presumably get her food in a canteen or something equivalent. I think Halls is what she calls the place where she sleeps but I didn't ask her for details as I don't want her to think I don't understand university life. I've never met anybody who had ever been to one before so I have no idea what goes on in those places.

Maggie and Sheila would be eating and sleeping in the same room in their digs as they called their place, and would be sharing the kitchen and bathroom and the lav with all the other tenants in the house. Can you imagine? It sounded absolutely horrific to me. I do hope it is clean.

Rhys hardly gave Helen, who was the last one to leave, time to get to the station before he commandeered the girls room. He moved their stuff into his box room at breakneck speed, not at his usual sloth like pace, and dumped most of it on the floor for me to sort out.

'And what about when they come home, where are they supposed to sleep?' I asked him.

'They are hardly likely to come at the same time are they now they've got shot of each other, and I doubt if that will be very often. There's no problem, 'cos they can sleep in my old room.' What a hurtful thing to say; he makes it sound as if they don't love me at all. Perhaps I'm kidding myself that they do? They certainly didn't hang about once they had a chance to leave.

In no time at all Rhys had obliterated the pretty floral wall paper in the girls' room with posters of jazz musicians such as Ronnie Scott, Humphrey Littleton, and Chris Barber, who seem to be all the rage with the young ones now, and there were also posters of sports cars, and near naked girls covering the rest of any wall space that was left. I thought he was far too young for that sort of thing, but Colin told me it was normal for boys of his age

'We used to have pictures of girls in various states of undress all-round the barracks when I was in the army. Colin told me so it's not just the young lads who like them, men love them too. Surely you remember Jane in the Daily Mirror? She had clothes on in the comic strip. But not in the posters we had in the barracks' he said. I can't say I was happy at the idea of Colin looking at that sort of girl as I might come out badly in comparison.

Rhys also put a huge KEEP OUT notice on the door, and once he had done that, he slipped back into his sloth like behaviour of doing nothing. I had to creep in when he was at school to clean the pit he had turned the room into, but I made sure **not** to tidy it, which would have caused a major eruption from him. I ring the girls every week hoping to speak to them, but it is not always easy. The communal phones are in the hall in Maggie's house, and Helen's is in the hall of wherever her room is, and nobody ever answers them. Neither of the girls makes any attempt to call each other, so I have to persist in trying to speak to them each week, and tell them what the other one is doing otherwise they would never know. I finally got through to Maggie but I don't know why I bothered.

'Hello Maggie, I hope you are well?' I said to her.

'Course I am Mum but I'm very busy'.

'Have you rung your sister?'

'Why would I do that, what's wrong with her?'

'Nothing as far as I know, but she's your sister. Surely you want to know how she's getting on at university?'.

'Not particularly – anyway she never rings me'.

Maggie seemed to think that was a good enough reason not to have any contact with Helen. I think she said this to placate me. I then had a similar conversation with Helen but I will never give up the idea of the girls bonding. I can dream can't I?

Chapter nine
Maggie 1963

Wow, what a super time to be alive and young. There is an air of excitement and change in the air that is almost tangible. London is emerging chrysalis like from its post war blues and the first buds of the change of life style that will swiftly follow were beginning to flower. All you old fogies better get used to it. **The kids are now in charge.**

Maybe my editor won't take kindly to the reference to old fogies as they are the mainstay of our readership. Better change it. I was writing my column, but kept stopping to look out of the window at the sunshine and the daffodils in the flower boxes in the window sills of the offices opposite the COURIER building. All that gorgeous yellow; it gave me a great feeling.

There are photographs of a girl of sixteen from Neasden (of all the dreary places in London to come from) called Twiggy. Her face is on every bill board and every magazine cover from Vogue to Jackie. She has a short sculptured blond hair style, and wears simple mini dresses, a completely new look that I can't imagine anyone over twenty five wearing successfully, but looks stupendous on a teenager, and is proof of the dramatic change in fashion waiting for all you young 'uns. Grab it girls, make your statement. No more twin sets and pearls—thank God. Was there ever such an ageing style that turned girls from leaving school into middle aged women overnight? Long live Twiggy, that's the look you need to achieve.

Perhaps I should scrap twenty five and not specify any age, and I wonder how many readers we have in Neasden? Yeah, I better rephrase it. I must interview Twiggy soon before she is no longer the face of today. That can change overnight in these fast moving times.

I was excited about the period I was living in, and grateful that I was around and a part of it. Pop groups were taking over the music charts once the property of crooners and girl singers bemoaning their lost loves. New restaurants such as the Spaghetti House, displayed posters say We NEVER serve Spaghetti on toast; the only way the Brits had eaten it before. Experimental theatre groups were springing up in pubs, and grotty halls in unfashionable parts of the capital. Joan Littlewood purchased the derelict Theatre Royal in Stratford, East London, where the actors painted and restored the pace in between performances and their productions were beginning to find their way to the West End. Clothes were getting wilder and more colourful by the minute and as for me, little 'ole Maggie, no hoper, according to my sister and mother, at twenty five was riding high with my own column called Maggie's London in one of the top National newspapers and with a big pay cheque to go with it. I get tickets for all the first nights in the theatres, the openings of the myriad of new restaurants springing up everywhere, and invitations to the fashion shows of all the new YOUNG designers like Mary Quant, and I get a chance to use my photographic skills taking pictures of the new generation of beautiful people, to use them in my column. It seems that the country is finally throwing off the wartime restraints and learning to live again. Could life be any better for me? No way.

Chapter ten
Helen 1961 - 1963

I achieved my aim to get a first class degree from university, and then passed the Civil Service entrance exam with flying colours, so my career path was set. and so was Richard's. I was elated. I'd met Richard Capstic at university, and he also wanted to be in the Civil Servise, and I'd decided he would make a suitable husband for me; he doesn't know it yet, but give me time.'

Unfortunately I have had to move back to my parent's house, as the rents in central London are extortionate. To add insult to injury, I have to sleep in the box room because Rhys has commandeered my old bedroom. I demanded that Mum should make him give it back to me, but she wouldn't as she said I will be off as soon as it suits me, and Rhys would still be with them and it wasn't fair to keep moving him about.

'How do you know he won't move out?' I asked her.

'Can you imagine him coping on his own?' No, 'course you can't because he would never be able to look after himself. He even has trouble making a cup of tea. You know it's *where's the tea Mum, I can't find the sugar.*' So I end up making it for him.' Mum said.

She's probably right. He will live here until he marries and beyond if he can get away with it, then some poor girl will take over from Mum doing everything for him, the lazy little sod. He's made no attempt to find a job. I think Dad would like to give him notice to quit just to make him get off his backside, Mum won't let that happen.   'He would end up sleeping under a bridge with all those down and outs wouldn't he?' she said, and I couldn't argue with her because I know she's right, but I was not best pleased.

Mum was shrieking up the stairs Helen, Helen come quickly, Maggie's on the tele.

'She's what -- doing what? for God's sake?'

'Something about violence in the home I think. Quickly love or you will miss her my excited mother called up the stairs. It was humiliating enough having to move back home because with all my qualifications I still couldn't afford the rent for anywhere in a decent neighbourhood, and now my sister – who is nowhere near as intelligent as I am, earns far more than I do, and is not even as attractive as I am -- and - and – she is fatter than me, so why is she is being asked her opinion on television?

'Doesn't she look pretty?' cooed my Mother.

'I think she looks common', I told her and she did looked at me a bit quizzically. She usually sides with me against Mag's. But she was right, she did look pretty. She must have had a makeover with her Afro hair and ethnic dress she had found a style that really suited her. I'm the one who was meant to succeed, while she was pontificating on a prestigious television programme. Something has to change in my life. I simply cannot have her overtaking me anymore. That's not how it is meant to be.

Chapter eleven
Maggie 1963

I've done something really stupid and embarrassing. It's nine in the morning and I have just arrived home. I woke up in this very comfortable bed in a beautiful flat that had obviously been designed by somebody famous, having no recollection of the previous evening or who the man standing over by the windows is, or how the hell I got here.

'Good morning Maggie, and how are you feeling this bright and sunny day?' he said. He knows my name. Shit, who is he?

'Sorry who are you, and where am I?' Oops, I didn't phrase that well I did I?

His reply confirmed it.

'That's rather ungracious of you. I'm the guy you slept with last night, and I thought you enjoyed our coupling as much as I did, but if you don't remember anything about it that makes the whole thing a waste of time' he replied huffily. Oh dear, I've damaged his ego.

'Sorry that was ill mannered of me. I wasn't really awake when you spoke to me' I said, hoping that would do the trick and placate him.. I didn't want to knock his confidence anymore, as looking around the bedroom he was obviously worth a bob or two and could be worth nurturing.

'Do you want any breakfast?' he asked. No I don't, I just want to get out of here I thought.

'Just a cup of coffee will do thanks'. I replied. What day was it, should I be at work? Confused thoughts ran through my head and I swore to myself, not for the first time that, I would never drink again.

'Where's your loo?' I asked.

'Which one?' He replied sarcastically. 'Any one, I need a pee.' I responded grumpily. I peered out of the bathroom window hoping I would recognise where I was. Eureka! Just along the road I could see Battersea Bridge. I could creep out of this place and walk home from here. A phone rang, or rather several phones rang. They seemed to be in every room. What luxury! 'Piers Roger's he answered with authority.

Oh shit!. He's my new boss. Am I still employed? I felt a blush rising from my toes to the top of my head. I'd never met him before. He wasn't part of the work force; he was the new **owner**. What drivel did I subject him to last night I wondered? Death would be welcome at this point.

'Do you want a lift anywhere?' He asked me without a great deal of enthusiasm. 'No thanks' I replied, 'I can walk home as I live not too far away from here. I need to go home for a shower and a change of clothes. Thank you very much for a super evening.'

'I thought you couldn't remember it.'

'I won't forget you Maggie' he said sarcastically. What did he mean by that?

OK if it was as compliment, but it worried me the way he said it. I think it's a threat, and as a newspaper owner -- the newspaper I work for --, he could do me a lot of harm. Well there's nothing I can do about it now.

When I arrived home, I told Sheila about my episode with Piers in a jocular way, but she didn't seem to think it funny.

'I think my drinking is getting out of hand.' I confessed to her.

'You can say that again, you actually talk rubbish most of the time. I am amazed you can still write your column,' she countered.

I was taken aback, and was about to deny what she had said — then stopped myself. We had known each since we were five, and she had every right to criticise me if that's what she thought, but was I really that bad?

Perhaps Gerry will help me cut down, but then he matches me drink for drink so he's not going to be much use is he? I said to her.

I had met Gerry McIntyre nearly two years ago at some BBC do or other, and we had become a sort of couple ever since – baring one or two little sorties off the straight and narrow. The trouble with him – or maybe me -- was he was just too good to be true. He was handsome, very posh, a member of the Anglo Irish landed gentry and therefore loaded, plus he was a top journalist at the Beeb. He was good fun, and he was potty about me. I loved swanning into a bar on his arm, and seeing all the girls looking at me with envy: consequently I wasn't really sure whether I was in love with **him** or a fairy tale prince, or even if I was in love at all. Maybe I was just besotted because of the glamour he exuded. Any way, it didn't really matter because I was having a great time.

'He's a real catch, you could do a lot worse'. Sheila, a big fan of his, said.

'Are you trying to get rid of me? Won't you miss me at a little bit? I like living here and I don't want to catch anyone yet. He's terribly posh you know, and I am not sure I can deal with that on a long term basis, also I might miss out on lots of things being tied to him' I responded.

'Miss out with what? Another episode like yesterday's debacle she quizzed me. Who else are you hoping to hook, Prince Charles? You really couldn't do better than Gerry.'

'Maybe you are right. I'll talk to him about moving in, if you don't mind. You will need someone else to share the rent with wont you?'

'Don't worry about that, I just want you to sort yourself out, and I think a change of lifestyle might be the answer' my best friend in the whole world told me.

Chapter twelve
Helen 1962

The job I am doing at the Ministry could be done by a sixteen year old school leaver, not by someone with my academic achievements.

'I'm wasted there,' I complained to my Mother. I was surprised when she responded, 'Well darling, it's up to you to change things.' Not the reply I expected from her. She has never seen the need to change anything – except Maggie's and my behaviour towards each other, but even she could see that everything was changing with this new exciting can do atmosphere that was sweeping the country. Seeing Maggie on television had really riled me, and I am determined to turn my life around somehow.

I had experienced how the Civil Service worked and I realised neither myself nor Richard, both from working class backgrounds, were ever going to go far in our chosen profession as any promotion going would go to ex public school pupils with Oxbridge degrees, or the sons and daughters of the well connected. A plan was needed to change my life and I wanted it to include Richard. I hadn't made the progress I had hoped for with him yet, so he would need a bit of persuading to uproot him. I went into attack mode.

'Let's go up to town on Saturday, have a bite to eat and maybe see a show' I exclaimed. He looked a bit taken aback at first, and then enthusiastically agreed.

'OK, Why not?' he said. Phew!

Now I have to overwhelm him with my idea so he doesn't have time to prevaricate. I dragged him into Joe Lyons in the Strand where we ordered cheese on toast. (Not all of London had fully taken in the changes in the food offer expected now, Lyons being one of them) but considering the bombshell I was about to drop on him, I thought somewhere conventional would settle him before I struck.

'Neither of us is making any progress in our jobs' I challenged him,' so what do you think about packing them in, then me retraining as a teacher and you – possibly studying finance or the law? If we hurry up and get married in the next four weeks we will qualify for a tax rebate to give us a good start financially.' I announced very quickly, not giving him a chance to interrupt my flow.

When he had regained his composure after having choked on his blue cheese, (being a cheddar man it was a first for him as he was feeling adventurous) he had embarrassed me by spitting most of it out all over the table, bringing an army of waiters rushing over to mop him down.

'What brought that on, the marriage bit in particular?' I ignored his question and continued to tell him my plan.

'We will need to move into Central London and rent a room. We won't be able to afford a flat at first while we are retraining, but we will save on the fares we are spending just to get to work by continuing to live here in the suburbs.

'What on earth will we live on?' He interjected, cautious as ever.

'There are grants available you know.'

He stared at me for a minute or two, and then his expression changed.

'Really?' He paused for a minute or two, then banged his fist on the table causing further disruption and embarrassment to me, but it was worth it because I had won.

'We'll do it. I'll get a marriage licence tomorrow' he told me with great enthusiasm. I wonder how long it would have taken him to ask me to marry him if I hadn't sprung it on him. We could have been one of those couples who are engaged for five years or more, and then split up.

Poor Mum, I don't think this was the marriage ceremony she had envisaged for either of her daughters. She wanted me overdressed in yards of white lace with an orange blossom head dress, in church of course, and the reception in that ghastly hotel in the high street she loves so much with dozens of Dad's northern relatives that I have never met. Instead she had to put up with the Town Hall Registry Office, with a couple of old school friends of mine as witnesses and a quick cup of tea afterwards before we left for our newly acquired bedsitting room in Paddington.

Perhaps Maggie will have a proper wedding, I mused. Somehow I doubt it.

Chapter thirteen
Maggie 1963

I am now ensconced in this gloriously smart Notting Hill flat with Gerry, and life is great. Now I am not rampaging round the bars and clubs around Fleet Street, I have cut down my drinking considerably. We indulge in what I call civilized boozing; you know a small aperitif before dinner, wine with it and a couple of brandies when we are curled up on the sofa watching television – or in the bath together surrounded by sweet smelling candles.. Beautifully decadent, that's of course if he is not reading the late night news which he does occasionally. Then I am stuck in the flat on my own for hours, and if I am honest, I am inclined to knock it back a bit.

I met his Mother today and we hit it off straight away. Extraordinary really as we couldn't be more different. She is around five foot seven or eight towering over my five foot four and there's the age difference as well. She is a very grand lady, a product of generations of breeding, and I am only a suburban working class girl, but none of that seemed to matter. However, his father Bertram is completely different kettle of fish. He's an old style Civil Servant, the sort who ends up with a title, and he is remote and unapproachable, and he made it clear he was not impressed with me. Fortunately he stays at his club when he is in London overnight whereas Jennifer stays with us. Jennifer told me to expect other ancient aunts to appear from time to time as they also stayed at the flat when they were in London for a concert or the theatre. I must have looked a bit surprised so she explained the flat didn't belong to Gerry; it was part of the family property portfolio. He hadn't told me that, but gave me the impression he owned it. Should that worry me?

Sure enough, just as Jennifer had predicted just one week after I met her, the front door was opened and an elderly autocratic lady was standing in the hall arguing with the cab driver over her fare.

'Things have changed since you lived here darlin' and that's what it costs now so pay up.' the cab driver demanded. She spotted me.

'Who are you child?' Not waiting for an answer she ordered me to pay the taxi driver, and as it was not the sort of voice you disobeyed, I paid up.

'And you are?'

'I'm Gerry's girlfriend Maggie.'

'Girl friend? Interesting; I always thought he was one of those.'

'Those what?' I asked her now totally confused.

'Poofters dear. They all are at the BBC aren't they? Bring my bags along. Which room am I in?'

'I'm not sure; I didn't know you were coming.'

'Nor did I, but I had a sudden urge to see my sister in law,' the stranger announced.

'Let's see if the blue room is ready for habitation shall we? What larks eh?' she said.

When Gerry arrived home I told him 'There's a strange lady in the flat. She had a key. Who is she?' I inquired.

'God, I forgot to tell you. Whenever any of my relatives come to town for a concert or the theatre, they stay here. Sorry darling, rather odd arrangement I agree, but the flat is part of the family property portfolio, so it doesn't really belong to me.'

'I know it's not your flat. Jennifer told me.'

'Did she? Oh sorry darling, I should have told you myself.' A bit late I thought.

'Your aunt thinks you are a poofter,' I told him laughing as I did.

'That'll be Aunt Sybil, my father's sister. She's quite mad and thinks anyone in the arts or the BBC is bound to be homosexual. Is she in the blue room?'

'Yes, I carried her case in for her.'

'I bet she ordered you to carry her bags. She's quite an authoritarian. I'll pop in to see her'. he said, grinning from ear to ear.

The next day I breezed into the news room to find the place buzzing, but not in a good way.

'What's happened I asked?'

'Kennedy has been shot and may not survive' one of my mates replied. My happy bubble had been burst. The world had narrowly avoided a nuclear war with the Bay of Pigs debacle just a few months before, and now this tragedy.

Chapter fourteen
Helen 1965

Things are definitely looking up for us and we both feel we did the right thing giving up our jobs and retraining. Living in a bedsitting room was the bit I was dreading most of all, but even that has turned out to be fun. Most of the other occupants of the house are people like us who have moved into the Capital to take advantage of opportunities not readily available in the small towns that some of them come from, and we have made new friends. We now have a social life as well; something sadly lacking when we were living our parents homes. I am retraining as a teacher and with my first class degree I know I will land a well-paid position in a private school as soon as I qualify. Richard is attending lectures at the LSE (London School of Economics) and loving it.

Just as I anticipated we have both graduated for the second time with high marks. Richard was immediately offered a very good job in a bank with a chance of promotion within six months, and I have landed a dream job in a top private school near Hyde Park for the children of the rich and famous. Now I am finally meeting the sort of people I always wanted to mix with. We had put a deposit on a flat in Fulham, an area that had been badly run down, but its borders adjoin Chelsea, and Chelsea is where **everybody** wants to live. I phoned Mum and told her.

'That's not a very nice area', she observed. Mum can be so negative sometimes. I told her the properties are cheaper, -- <u>much</u> cheaper there, and it's becoming a very desirable neighbourhood and we will make a killing when we come to sell it. I don't think she believed me. Richard, as cautious as ever thought we ought to save more money before committing ourselves to a mortgage. He's a bit of stick in the mud sometimes and doesn't share my ambition. He's very self-effacing too, which can be either charming or irritating depending on the circumstances. He often needs a push in the right direction as he doesn't seem to realise we have moved up the social scale now and we need to change certain aspects of our lives in order to mix with the right sort of people. He was very cross with me when he overheard me talking to Jeremy, our new neighbour, and I told him that my father was a business advisor.

'What does Colin do then? Advise customers how to put money in their meters?' Richard questioned sarcastically. He really doesn't understand. Jeremy would not be impressed that my father worked for the Gas Board and Richards's father was only a bus driver.

I've met a couple of new friends on my bus journey to work, Lorraine and Trish. They have persuaded me to join the Conservative Party. I told Richard and tried to get him to join too.

.'Lorraine and Trish? Who on earth are they, and why on earth would I want to join the Tory party?'

'The girls are new friends of mine.' Richard was very sharp with me.

'Friends, I don't think you know the meaning of the word anymore.' he snapped.

'I really don't care for this social climbing side of you Helen, and I cannot understand why we have to join any political party? We have never been politically biased in favour of any party, and both our fathers are members of the Labour party and would be mortified if we joined the Tories' he complained.

'Well we don't have to tell them do we? I said. Richard glared at me. I really don't care what either of them thinks. They are the past and we are the future, but I won't say that to Richard. I'm sure he wouldn't approve. I carried on smiling at him.

'We will meet the right kind of people, at their social functions.' I told him smiling sweetly. 'There you go again' he said 'the right kind of people; that's the sort of remark I mean. Who do you think **we** are? We are just a couple of working class kids who were born at the right time, and have had opportunities our parents could have dreamt of; and as for your social functions, you mean FUND raising shin digs don't you? That's going to cost us a pretty penny. I thought we were going to take it easy with our cash and use it to improve the flat' he muttered.

Oh dear, I really have rattled his cage. I didn't ask him to fill in his application form for the Conservatives; I did it for him and forged his signature. When he received some literature from them I told him he automatically became a member as my husband. He glared at me then binned it. I heard him telling his mother on the phone that he disliked my social climbing and that I needed to get off my high horse and return to planet earth pretty soon, as he was getting a bit fed up with it. Perhaps I had better go softly softly for a while as I don't want to lose him. I need a husband to fit in with my future plans, and besides, I really love him.

Chapter fifteen
Maggie 1966

It wasn't long after I had moved in with Gerry before he started talking about marriage. That was definitely a step too far for me and I made endless excuses as to why this was a bad idea, but I kept my real reason from him which was mainly because he was so out of my league as far as our backgrounds were concerned. He didn't think this was a problem, nor did Jennifer when he told her that he wanted to marry me, but their world was totally alien to me. It was fine here in London where most of our friends were journalists: but when we attended one of his old school friend's wedding, I felt like a fish out of water. But bit by bit they wore me down and I said maybe—I'm still prevaricating though.

Because of all this talk about marriage, talking to Jennifer one day I cheekily asked her where did she meet Bertram as they seemed such an odd couple with only their class in common..

'Oh the usual way at the High Society cattle market.' She replied.

'The what?' I asked her laughing out loud.

'The Debutante Balls, where the eligible daughters of the aristocracy and those who can afford to buy their way into the coven, parade their nubile offspring in front of suitable young men to bare the fruit of their loins at – hopefully — a later date. However there are a few mishaps and hastily arranged nuptials every season. The whole thing is designed to keep the money within the acceptable families as it is not safe to let these young bucks loose; as they might marry outside of the approved circle and bring in the wrong type.'

'Like me you mean' I giggled.

Poor Jennifer, realising what she had said, blushed and tried to talk her way out of her faux par.

'Personally I think it would be a good thing as there is an awful lot of inbreeding within our social circle – how can I put this politely? – No I won't bother—idiots and lunatics abound within our circle. Their lack of brains heavily disguised by good manners and upper class accents.'

'I am pleased you think that way as I will definitely supply the common touch to any children Gerry and I may have'. I told her.

Help! I shouldn't have said that as it made it sound as if I had decided to marry Gerry. I hastily dived in with a question, hoping she hadn't noticed my slip of the tongue and asked Jennifer if there were any lunatics tucked away in their family.

'You bet there are. We can trace the family back to Oliver Cromwell, when the estates in Ireland were given to the family, but before that the trail gets mixed up between the rackety Irish lot, and the stuck up English ones, and there are definitely a few members who seemed to have been suspiciously kept out of the limelight. Fortunately that gene, or whatever it is that causes the problem seems to have died out in the McIntyres in the last fifty years.'

Jennifer was in London to meet a friend to attend a concert at the Wigmore Hall, but her friend had cried off as she had a heavy cold.

'Why don't you join me?' she invited. I had never been to a classical concert in my life, but shrewd lady that she was, I bet she knew that. Maybe she was training me to enjoy the tastes of the educated classes before I married Gerry?

Perhaps she is not quite as egalitarian as she appears to be? Anyway I loved the concert, Mozart's piano concerto in something or other. Must check the programme to make sure so as not to slip up when I talk about it.

I had a night out with Sheila and told her about my concerns over the marriage.

'You would be mad if you let him off the hook. Go for it, you can always get a divorce if it doesn't work out.' she said.

'I don't want to marry thinking I can get a divorce; I want to marry for life' I told her, a bit peeved that she would think that way, but then I thought about her parents' marriage and understood why she didn't have much faith in the happy ever after. A few weeks later I finally agreed to marry him still worrying about the class difference, but he brushed that to one side.

'You silly goose he said to me. I love you lots and lots and that's what is important, and the family will see you have made your way in the world and become successful, and will become even more so in the future.' I was worried. Is that what he expects? I suppose as he would as he comes from a family of achievers. Perhaps I need to become more ambitious? Oh 'gawd – Pressure, pressure!

'You'd better get used to my full name before we marry.' he said. 'I can't have you collapsing with laughter at the altar. 'It's Algernon Gerard Tristan Pasco MacIntyre.

I tried not to laugh in case it offended him but I failed – and exploded, falling off the chair in helpless giggles.

'Am I to become Mrs that lot? I asked him.

'Fraid so my darling,' he replied also laughing.

A few weeks later we had a show biz style wedding at Caxton Hall with lots of journalists and BBC types in attendance as well as members of Gerry's family, even Piers Rogers was there. My Editor had brought him along. I wanted to curl up and die when I spotted him.

'Maggie, I don't think you have met our new owner Piers Rogers have you?' Curtis asked.

'No I haven't – lovely to meet you' I stuttered.

'I am delighted to finally make your acquaintance young lady having long been an admirer of your work. You have a racy modern style that appeals to our younger readers, a market I intend to capitalise on. Best wishes for your future.

I've known Gerry and his family for many years' he smirked. Was that a threat? It sounded like it. What a bastard I thought as I smiled sweetly at him and thanked him for his kind words.

There were photographs of Gerry and me in all the Nationals the following day and I realised Mum and Dad would see them. They would find out about their errant daughter's nuptials and they would be desperately upset at their exclusion. I was ashamed of myself for not asking them, but my excuse to myself was I thought they would be uncomfortable with the high flyers and aristos on the guest list as they wouldn't understand the social circle I now moved in. This was true, but I could have given them the chance to decline the invitation themselves. I had lied to Gerry and Jennifer telling them my parents lived in Spain, and they were not in the best of health at the moment, so they had sadly decided not to travel. I feel ashamed every time I think about it because neither Gerry nor his Mother were snobs, and would have been furious with me if they had known about my lie. They didn't care about peoples backgrounds because they were grand enough not to be bothered by people's origins. Anyway, Gerry was a member of the Labour party as was my Dad, not a Tory as you would have expected, and he had ambitions to be an MP one day. The real reason was ME.

I am disgusted with myself to admit that I would have been embarrassed by my very respectable suburban parents, but I didn't want my mother interfering with arrangements for the reception, which she would naturally have wanted to do, so I didn't ask them. All of this was a load of rubbish. The truth was I was behaving like a first class snobby cow and I was thoroughly ashamed of myself, and had no idea how I could make reparations to them.

Feeling guilty, I telephoned them from the airport before we boarded the plane to Delhi to start our honeymoon. We were touring as much of India that we could manage in three weeks, which was all the time we had managed to get off work. Unsurprisingly they were really angry with me.

'Why didn't you tell us? Why didn't you invite us? Are you ashamed of us or something?' Mum pleaded.

'No honestly I lied. I'm really sorry Mum, but it was a rushed job and ...'she stopped me in my tracks.

'Well it didn't look a rushed job to me; in fact it looked a very well planned affair. Did you know your sister was married a few weeks ago too?'

I did because Mum had already told me, but I let her go on.

'That was a proper rushed affair unlike yours, with only a cup of tea to toast them with before they caught the train to Paddington and their one roomed home, if you can call it that. Very disappointing but at least we were invited.'

'Is Helen pregnant then having such a hurried wedding?' I asked .trying to divert her from my feeble excuses.

'No she's not' she answered crossly. I could ask the same question of you, as you claim your wedding was rushed too so you tell me.' Dad then snatched the phone from Mum and gave me a major bollocking.

'It was unthinkable of you not to invite us to one of the most important days of your life. Didn't it occur to you or your sister, that the dream of any mother is to see their daughters married and happy, but neither of you gave her a second thought did you? I'm ashamed of the pair of you' he shouted and he slammed the phone down on me. I burst into tears and had to tell another lie to Gerry as to why I was upset. I resolved to make it up to them as soon as I could and introduce them to my new husband. Tricky, as they are supposed to be living in Spain. How am I going to get over that one?

Chapter sixteen
Helen 1966

Just when I was feeling pleased with my life, my cow of a sister has to spoil everything for me again. There are pictures of her all over the Nationals on her wedding day at Caxton Hall, laughing her silly head off. Mum had told me she had a boyfriend, but didn't tell me it was HIM, that dishy BBC man. How did she manage to land a guy like that? And that dress must have cost a fortune. Did Mum go to the wedding? She didn't tell me she had. I must give her a ring.

'How was the wedding Mum? I presume you went.'

'No we bloody didn't. We were not invited. Too common I suppose to introduce to her new posh friends.'

Oh dear, poor old Mum, that's really shocking of Maggie not to ask Mum and Dad. That'll put her in their bad books. Good, that might be to my advantage. I know my wedding wasn't up to much, but at least I invited them. I commiserated with her.

'What a bitch Mum. Who does she think she is?'

I sound like Richard when he criticises me. His latest accusation is he thinks I have probably always been a closet snob but didn't have anything to be snobby about before university. Maybe Maggie and I have that in common—we are BOTH snobs, otherwise why did she exclude mum and dad?

Richard had only worked at bank just over a year when an amazing opportunity presented itself. A failing small bank had come on the market. Carlos and Simon, friends he had met at the LSE (London School of Economics) had put in a bid for it and asked Richard to join them in the venture. I heard him tell his father Reg he wasn't going to discuss it with me because I would say yes for all the wrong reasons and would realise if he joined his friends, he would become a Company Director and that would give me something to brag about to my new found friends, and this would override any sensible advice I might give him.

Richard's dad, phoned me to tell me what he had said because he was worried our marriage was breaking down. It really upset me that Richard felt that he could no longer trust me to give him an objective view of his plans as I do love him, and would hate our marriage to fall apart.

When I finally managed to get him to discuss his plans, I told him to do whatever he thought was the right thing for HIM, to go ahead and do it, and not to worry about what I thought as I would support him whatever he decided. That did the trick and he kissed me. It's been a long time since he's done that. The three of them, Simon, Richard, and Carlos, with a little help from Carlos's Spanish uncle, managed to raise the finance to purchase what had once been a small prestigious banking company run by men from old families and old money Richard told me. These guys thought life was going to return to the old order exactly the way it was before the war, but they should have guessed when Churchill's Tories lost the General Election in July 1945 that the country wanted change; but they didn't, hence they were unprepared for the upheaval taking place in the financial world which, is why they went under giving Richard and his friends a chance to bring it up to date.

I went along with him to see the premises and met Carlos who was giving a spirited rendition of 'Were in the money' and dancing the Flamenco on a table. Richard said he was actually from Tunbridge Wells, but liked everyone think he was from Barcelona as it sounded more exotic. Another snob.

Richard could read me like a book, as I <u>did</u> love telling my friends my husband was a Company Director, omitting telling them there were two others and it was a very small company. I even telephoned Maggie to tell her, but Mum had got there first.

'Why do we still play this pathetic one-up-manship game all the time? It really is demeaning.

Then, all too soon in our new life I found I was pregnant. I wasn't ready for babies – **we** weren't ready for babies. I was going to sidle off and have an abortion somewhere, not that I had any idea how to go about it, but Richard had guessed. My throwing up every morning gave him a clue, and he was thrilled, so there was nothing I could do to stop the inevitable. There's only one bedroom in the flat so I suppose we will have to sell up and find somewhere more suitable for a brat. Pity, as I like living here.

Chapter seventeen
Maggie 1967

A few months after we were married, out of the blue I received an offer to apply for a job as a roving reporter for Alex McDonald Productions Ltd who made documentary films for the major television companies, with a contract and a big fat salary to go with it.

'Gerry, Gerry I called, Can you believe it?' I was dancing round the table in my excitement. He was thrilled, but not overtly so. It would go without saying his wife would be expected to progress in her chosen career as I had married into a family of achievers, which was quite a lot to live up to for mere mortals like me.

After meeting with Alex and the staff in their studio come office they offered me the job. I was thrilled and gave in my notice at the COURIER. The editor was delighted for me as were my colleagues as they felt it was an opportunity I had to grab to extend my CV, and off we went to the pub to celebrate. When we got back to the newsroom, Piers Rogers was there to greet us. Why was he here? He usually left us to get on with things without any interference from him? I was apprehensive and had a feeling in the pit of my stomach that it was something to do with me.

'Come into the office Maggie, I need to speak to you' he commanded. I was right. He was gunning for me.

'I believe you have had an attractive offer from Alex McDonald and intend to leave the COURIER. Not a good idea.' He smirked. 'I have plans for the future of the paper, and they include you, so I can't have you running away can I? You pull in the younger readers and this is an untapped market for the dailies, and one I intend to develop.'

'But I ...

'No buts Maggie. I just might tell Gerry about your drunken little mishap with me weeks before he was about to marry you .Did you tell him? No, I bet you didn't. I don't think his family would be best pleased to see the story on the front page of the News of the World do you? Obviously I know the Editor very well, and I am sure he would love to publish such a juicy story. His family may appear to be very trendy and modern, but scratch the surface of these old aristocratic families and they are still as traditional as they ever were when scandal hits the headlines. Believe me; you will be out of your marriage so fast your feet won't touch the ground. Capiche?

There's that bloody word again. I've no idea what the real meaning of it is, but I know whenever I hear it means Shut up and get on with whatever I've said, and argue with me at your peril.

'I will naturally give you an increase in your salary and status' he continued, but you can tell Alex McDonald you won't be taking the job. Revenge is sweet my dear and I have waited a long time to execute it. That will teach you to belittle me' and with that he left the office grinning.

What on earth could I say or do? I love Gerry with all my heart, so I had to tell him I had turned down the job because I had been given a massive rise, and how I felt I owed my loyalty to the COURIER for giving me a chance early in my career. I'm not sure he believed me. I had a problem stopping the tears which I am sure my colleagues noticed as I told them I had decided to stay. I heard one of the journalist say to his mate 'What's she been up to. Has she been a naughty girl and he knows about it? I rushed into the loo and burst into tears. I had to contact Alex and tell him sadly I couldn't take the job at this point in time as I had been given a promotion at the COURIER, but thanked him for the offer and suggested maybe some time at in the future we could work together.

'Has that bastard Piers got something on you?' he asked. I was flustered.

'No no. It's just the timing is not good I said, but I don't think he believed me. I felt awful letting him down as he seemed such a nice guy.

Chapter eighteen
Helen 1966

The search for an affordable home to accommodate a new baby began and it very soon it became obvious that it was back to the bloody suburbs again, which really upset me. However there was one advantage. If we could find somewhere near Mum's then she could look after the baby and I could get back to work soon after giving birth. Without telling Richard I manoeuvred the house hunting in that direction, and we eventually found one we could afford.

Mum was delighted when I told her we were moving to a house just around the corner from my childhood home. Later I told her we couldn't really afford the mortgage unless I went back to work after I had the baby – a lie – and told her how expensive baby sitters were in the area – true. As I guessed she jumped at the chance of looking after her grandchild thank goodness.

I gave birth to a baby boy, Jason, two days after my twenty eighth birthday. He was enormous; nearly nine pounds and I swore never again would I go through that torture. If Richard wanted another child, he could give birth to it himself. I went back to work when he was six months old and good old Mum looked after him.

'I would have thought you would want to look after your first child yourself?' my Dad questioned, so I told him the same story I had told Mum that I needed the money, and that she had said how much she was looking forward to it.

'I'm not.' he said. 'I was hoping your mother and I could go away on holiday when we felt like it now you girls are married.'

Panic!

'What about Rhys? I countered, who will look after him?'

'For God's sake, he's twenty six years old, it's about time he looked after himself rather than having his mother dancing around him attending to his every whim. He should have left home years ago instead of running back here the minute things went wrong.'

Oh dear. I'm going to have to keep Dad sweet, as if he puts his foot down about Mum looking after Jason, all my plans will go awry.

Chapter nineteen
Maggie 1966 - 1967

'I wish you wouldn't drink so much. When you get pregnant you will have to stop you know'. Gerry demanded.

Pregnant? What's he talking about. Does he want babies? Well of course he does. He's the eldest son of an ancient family so he's obliged to produce an heir. Stupid me. The idea of having babies was not something that had crossed my mind. I will have to nip that idea in the bud for the time being at least.

'We haven't been married that long darling, so let's have some fun being Mr and Mrs before we start a family.' I simpered.

'We have been having fun for a couple of years already, so we mustn't leave leave it too long. You're getting a bit long in the tooth for your first child.'

Cheek! What's he talking about? I'm only twenty eight. First one? How many does he want?

Help .Forward planning doesn't appear to be my strong suit so this desire for baby has come as a big shock to me,

It's 1966 and London has finally thrown off the gloom of post-war depression and has really begun to swing and I want to continue to be part of it. The girls skirts are getting shorter by the day, and the boy's hair is getting longer The Beetles and the Rolling Stones have changed the music scene and the young ones are throwing themselves into the new world with abandonment , much to their parents horror. The old ideas of respectability have been tossed out of the window and right in middle of all this amazing excitement I've found out I was pregnant. Shit!'

I didn't tell Gerry for a few weeks hoping it would go away, but he noticed a bump growing on my usually flat stomach and guessed. He was over the moon.

'Right, we will have to move out of town and buy a house more suitable than this place.'

'Whatever for? 'I gasped. I loved our flat and never wanted to leave it.

'There's masses of room here and Holland Park is nearby, it'll be fine' I cried in desperation.

'We will keep it on in case either of us is working late on an assignment in town but we do need to move because of the child's future.'

My heart sank. I managed to delay the move for a while by pointing out how I difficult it would be to write my Maggie's London column stuck out in the wild wood.

'What do you mean, stuck out in the Wild Wood? We are not joining Toad and Badger you know. You're being silly and obdurate Maggie.' and with that Gerry walked out slamming the door as he stormed out of the flat.

Being in London turned out to be just as well as I went into early labour and was rushed into the private maternity ward in St Marys Hospital where the royal family have their heirs.

'You have been working too hard, that's why this has happened Gerry accused me. You should have taken more care of our child and moved to the country weeks ago.'

It was a difficult birth – what am I saying? –it was a horrendous experience. I yelled, I screamed I made a terrible fuss. I called Gerry every bad name I could think of, and believe me, I know a few. Finally our son was born and I called him Michael. I made this quite clear to Gerry and his mother that there would be no further discussion about this.

.'You can call him as many of those highfaluting names your family seem to prefer as his secondary names, but I want him to have a nice normal first one.' I said firmly.

'You're being a bit high handed. He's my son too remember, I would like to call him Tristan and I think Mummy wanted to call him Augustus'. Gerry said, rather peevishly I thought. Mummy? – Mummy! What's that all about? He's morphing into posh boy mode big time. Worrying! He and his brother usually call her Jen or aged parent. My tiny five pound scrap of a baby became Michael Tristan Augustus Septimus, Padraig MacIntyre. Poor kid lumbered with that lot.

Michael's early arrival in October delayed the move still further, and I hoped I would be able to prove to the Macintyre's that it would be fine bringing up a baby in London. Lovely Jennifer, who was usually on my side, persisted with the idea of moving to the country – because of the smog.

'We haven't had smog since the Clean Air Act was passed back in '56 I protested. Helen and I were brought up in London as were millions of other children, and it didn't do us any harm.'

'How do you know the long term effects of all that pollution on your lungs?' was her repost. I couldn't argue with that one could I? I was fighting a losing battle; better give in I suppose, but I was not happy. I don't know anything about the country, and more to the point, I have no interest in it whatsoever. I'm a city girl and I write about life in London, so why would I want to leave it? I don't think writing about gardening and pony clubs would interest my readers one little bit, and me even less.

Two weeks later

Before I could count to ten we were speeding along the M1 en route to Olney wherever that might be.

'Where are you taking me,' I pleaded with him.

'You will love it. We will be living in a beautiful house outside of Olney which is an absolute gem of a Georgian market town'

Petticoat Lane and Covent Garden are markets to me. What do I have in common with people who live in market towns? Bugger all.

'Why do we have to move so far out of London? You know I am not happy about the idea anyway and I thought WE were going to look for a house together, but it appears you and Mummy have decided MY future between you. Is my opinion of so little interest to you that you have decided on a house without consulting me at all? I yelled at him.' I was furious.

'The house is part of my family's property portfolio, and as the tenants lease is about to expire, Mummy suggested it might be ideal for us as she lives quite nearby.' Mummy has popped up again. Whatever happened to Jennifer, his lovely mother who I was so fond of – no, whom I loved? She's now called Mummy, and has become my adversary.

Chapter twenty
Helen 1967 - 68

My thirtieth birthday was looming and I decided that if we were going to have another child, this was the time to do it having forgotten my threat that Richard would have to bear a second child. Richard was earning a lot of money, making my salary unimportant towards our net income, so Richard agreed, so we went into baby production at every waking moment. Good fun actually: I wonder why we don't do it more often. Anyway all this activity paid off and I conceived within a few weeks.

Sophie was born on 8th of June, two days before my birthday, weighing in at nine pounds, ripping me to bits and resulting in heavens knows how many stitches.

'Another Gemini' my Mother shrieked with delight. I would have thought she'd had enough of those with Maggie and me. I think Mum must have broken every speed record going getting from

Frimley Green to St Stephens, as she appeared at my bedside almost as soon as I put the phone down, she was so excited. Dad was with her, not looking quite so pleased.

'I hope you are not expecting your Mother to look after Jason AND Sophie?' he barked almost before he reached my bed. I can't believe how selfish my family is, especially you, and I'm telling you right now I will only allow your Mother to look after your children for two days a week maximum.'

I'd just given birth to another enormous baby and was feeling shattered, so the last thing I wanted was my Dad lambasting me, so I burst into tears as that usually did the trick with him.

'Oh Colin, its OK dear. I will be happy to help out.' Mum piped up.

'No its not, you know how tired you get' he said to her sympathetically.

'You've taken advantage of her good nature for too long and 'yer mothers not getting any younger you know. I 'wanna to take her on 'oliday to Spain soon and. any way, it's about time you started to look after your own kids,' he said very firmly, 'and I will not allow her to continue to be on call every time it suits you.'

I couldn't believe what he had just said.

'Dad you cannot dictate what she can or can't do in this day and age. She's got a mind of her own, and it's up to her what she does or doesn't do. She loves looking after Jason'. I said through my tears.

'Not quite as much as you think young lady' he replied.

I suppose if I'm honest I had been pushing it a bit. Mum had been looking after Jason two days a week and I had started to leave him overnight as well. Mum actually looked pleased when Dad put his foot down.

'Please don't worry, of course we will find a nursery and we are just grateful you have been so kind looking after Jase for so long,' piped up Richard.

'Thanks lad. Come on lets go for a pint. I'll pick you up later Rene love' he said. Baby talk doesn't interest men for long does it? – it doesn't interest me for that long either, so I feigned tiredness so they would all go home and leave me alone wondering how much a nursery is going to cost.

Chapter twenty-one
Rene 1967

'What's this case in the hall' I called out to Rhys.

'I'm leaving home' he replied in that *I can't really be bothered to speak* drawl he uses just to irritate me. He probably thinks it's sophisticated, but it isn't -- it's just annoying.

'What are you talking about, where on earth are you going to live?'

'Away from those squalling brats: I need my sleep, and it's not possible with those monster babies in residence'

'Sophie and Jason don't live here and they don't always stay the night, and you get more than enough sleep anyway, 'cos you not only sleep all night but you sleep half the day as well and that is more than enough for any man.' I pleaded with him. 'How are you going to manage? You haven't got a job – you've **never** had a job – so what are you going to do for money, and how can you get work at your age without any references?'

'Mum there's another world out there that I've never experienced that I keep reading about. It's Swinging London. It's in my magazines and those columns Maggie writes. -- well we live in London but nothing swings round 'ere and I want to find it, so I'm off.'

Colin wasn't the least bit sympathetic saying he should have left years ago and it will be the making of him. I suppose I do have my grandchildren which is a blessing, although not always. Helen does leave them here longer than I would like sometimes. Rhys told me he was going to see if Maggie would put him up. I don't think he has much of a chance there. I can't think she will want him in her flat, which I believe is very smart. Not that I have ever seen it as she has never invited me to visit.

I made him promise to phone me after he had visited Maggie as I wanted to be sure he had somewhere to stay.' Much to my surprise he did, but it was not good news.

'I think she's ashamed of us Mum' he said. 'The moving vans were outside the house and she pushed me round the corner so fast that I couldn't meet Gerry. She did give me some money though and an address of a hostel nearby where I could stay. . Where does Helen live?'

'I don't think you will get much joy there either son. Go to the hostel and come home if you don't like it darling.' I pleaded with him.

He phoned me a couple of days later and told me I was wrong, about him not getting a job as he'd landed one in the first shop he walked into in Carnaby Street. They told him he had the right look to model their clothes as well as sell them, and took him on straight away.

'A bit 'poncey modelling clothes, but who cares if their paying me, and it's all happening here Mum.'

'What's all happening?' I stupidly asked which obviously annoyed him

'Swinging London of course' he snapped and then hung up on me.

Chapter twenty-two
Maggie 1967

The day before the move, my lies about the whereabouts of my parents caught me out. Jennifer couldn't understand why my mother hadn't flown over from Spain the minute I had given birth to Michael, and I was running out of excuses as to why she couldn't come. In the end I burst into tears (I have been known to use tears to gain sympathy) and blurted out the whole shameful episode to her as to why I hadn't invited them to the wedding and their anger with me when they saw all the press coverage the following day, and how disgusted I was with myself to exclude them the way I had

'You silly girl, do you honestly think we would have cared what your parents do for a living? Gerry is obviously in love with you, and you seem to be so happy together that's all that concerns me as a parent. Phone them straight away and tell the good news about Michael and invite them to the new house to stay as soon as possible, and you must tell Gerry without delay'. Jennifer chided.

When he finally turned up Jen told him 'Maggie has something to tell you, I'll give Michael his bath to give you time to talk.' I didn't know how to start so I burst into tears (again – I do overplay this card) and told him through my sobs what an absolute bitch I had been by telling lies about why my parents couldn't come to our wedding. It was really because they are very ordinary working class people, and I thought they would be overwhelmed by our friends, and if I'm being honest, I thought they might embarrass me if yo'

'Darling don't upset yourself, I hate to see you cry (that's why I did it) I am sure they will forgive you, how could they not as they must love you as much as I do,' he assured me. I think he was so relieved I wasn't going to leave him over the imminent move that it hadn't really sunk in what I had confessed to, but later that evening he gave me some odd looks which worried me. Denying your parents is a pretty despicable thing to do, especially when they have done nothing to deserve it. Is this the first chink in our fantastic relationship? I do hope not. Any doubts I had about whether I loved him or not, have been totally dispelled since we started living together, and it would break my heart if we split.

I rang Mum and Dad that evening and told them about Michael and the move to the country and I was informed very frostily that Helen had a daughter Sophie in June. That was a surprise as I didn't see her as the mother of two. She's far too selfish to be a good mum. Maybe I am too? I hope not.

'They can play together when they are older.' Mum exclaimed enthusiastically. Don't think so! That would entail Helen and I speaking to each other in a friendly way and I can't see that happening any time soon.

Jennifer had organised moving day, and as you would expect from her, it all went smoothly. I hadn't actually been inside the new house can you believe, which pissed me off big time. When he originally took me to see it I was so furious with him, that I refused to get out of the car to go in. What about furniture I asked Gerry.

'Oh don't worry about that, it is already furnished was his response.

'So I don't even get a say in how my home is furnished?' I yelled at him.

'But your style, fun though it is, wouldn't suit the house.'

'Perhaps you would like me to pay rent on my so called home' I ranted at him, then you as the landlord you will give me -- the tenant, - a list of what I can and can't do in it.' I fumed. 'Do you realise I haven't been allowed any input whatsoever in this bloody move, and you wonder why I am so pissed off about the whole pantomime?' I screamed at him, and stomped off out into Notting Hill. My speech has become very rough lately because of my anger with the way I have been manipulated into this move. That won't go down well with the Macintyre's.

I would have like to have vanished all day so they would have to send out search parties for me, but that would have been childish as the moving van needs to leave by midday. As I turned the corner I saw Rhys about to ring the doorbell. As the Macintyre's didn't know of his existence that would have been another lie I would have to explain, so I grabbed him by the arm, and steered him round the corner away from the house, gave him some money and sent him off to the Hostel in

South Kensington. He looked bewildered at my actions as he thought he was going to be able to move in with Gerry and me. Then he grinned at me.

'You aint told 'im about me 'ave you?'

'Why should I? You have nothing in common with each other. Come to that, **we** haven't got anything in common other than our parents, so there's no chance of me putting you up even if we weren't moving away from London. Good luck and goodbye.' were my parting words to the lazy little slob.

Chapter twenty-three
Rene 1968

Maggie has finally invited me to her new home and to meet her husband and mother in law, who she seems to be very fond of. I was thrilled. It was quite a difficult place to get to, and we had to change trains three times. Fortunately Maggie met us at the station nearest to her home to drive us the last bit. I was quite excited about meeting Jennifer more than Gerry; I don't know why.

When we got there I couldn't believe my eyes when I saw the house. It was huge. Maggie told me it was a typical Regency manor house, worth a fortune, but that she hated living there stuck in the country. I didn't like to ask her what a Regency manor was but I told her she an ungrateful girl and told her Helen would be in heaven living here. Maggie looked upset and told I am not Helen; we are two different people as I have told you again and again, and, yes, I bet she'd love it. Just think how she would lord it over the locals playing the lady of the manor.

Then this very tall lady with a really cultured voice towered over me saying how delighted she was to finally meet me. She took me by surprise and I froze. I am only five foot two and she must have been about five foot nine. Maggie glared at me obviously cross that I was struck dumb.

'Mum this is Jennifer, Gerry's mother; Jen meet my parents Rene and Colin Sutherland she said very firmly,' glaring at me as she said it.

'Rene is a very pretty name, is it French by any chance?' Jennifer asked.

I felt I had to make up for my silence so I told her my Mother was French, and my father had met her when he was in France fighting in the Great War. Maggie smiled at me. Good! I've done something right. I will feel better when we all sit down and Jennifer is not looming over me.

Colin has recently become a Trade Union leader, and was no longer the shy quiet man he used to be and has become very bolshie, especially with posh people. So he shook her hand in a very dominating way. I was embarrassed, and Maggie didn't seem to be pleased either. This meeting was not going well. I really hadn't realised how Maggie's life had changed so completely. Her house overwhelmed me, and I couldn't wait to get away. Meeting my grandson was not a success either. What a strange little boy he is. I gave him a present, a fire engine that I thought he would like, but he looked at it oddly then threw it on the floor and ignored me, never making eye contact at all or saying anything to us. I thought he was very rude, and couldn't understand why Maggie let him get away with such bad behaviour. I had always stressed the importance of good manners to my children. She must have seen the expression on my face so then apologised.

'Sorry about that Mum', Maggie piped up. 'We think he has a problem with the way his brain is wired, and we are going to have him tested soon.'

How his brain is wired? What is that supposed to mean? Probably an excuse the gentry use to make excuses for their badly behaved children.. They wouldn't get away with that where we live. They would get a clip round the ear for being rude, and sent to bed without their tea. That would soon learn 'em.

We were supposed to be meeting Gerry as well but we didn't. He telephoned and I heard Maggie remind him that we were here, and could he please make an effort and get home early to make sure of meeting us. We were meant to be having supper together (another posh word meaning tea I suppose) and staying the night, but I had decided I wanted to leave as soon as possible, so we made our excuses and left early. I could tell Maggie was furious with me, and Jennifer looked disappointed. I heard Maggie apologising to Jennifer, and Jennifer apologising to Mag's, both of them concerned as to whose fault it was why we were leaving early.

Reflecting on the disastrous day I did think it might have been partly my fault, as I really didn't try to fit in and make Maggie proud of me which I had intended to do., If I am honest with myself, I think I was jealous of Maggie's relationship with her mother in law. She was never close to me like that. I'm her Mother. It's me she should confide in. Why doesn't she? Where did I go wrong?

Chapter twenty-four
Helen 1968

I am trying to take in what Richard has just told me; it was some convoluted story about the Fraud Squad interviewing him and his partners about a money laundering scheme they had been involved in.

'What the hell have you been up to?' I shrieked.

He used to tell me about his work at the bank, but to be honest with you I'd stopped listening as he explained what they were doing. I'm afraid my only interest in his job was the money and the prestige it gave me with my friends. Perhaps I should have listened to him more keenly and taken in what he was saying, then maybe I could have prevented whatever mess he'd managed to get himself in.

'Explain to me exactly what crime you and your idiot mates have committed?' I ordered him, hoping my good sense and intelligence would be able to mitigate some of the problems for them.

'We got involved with a Spanish company who persuaded us to join forces with them in a money laundering scam – only they didn't call it that at the time, and we naively went along with the scheme.'

How could they be so ignorant? They were all supposed to be bankers. Surely they could have recognised a scam when they saw one. I managed to hold my tongue as Richard was beginning to get emotional, and I wanted to hear the whole story before I berated him again.

'Go on, I'm listening' I encouraged him, but seething inside.

'OK. To simplify what we did; the Spaniards sold us a way of investing money in high interest schemes and pay very little tax on the returns. Simon and I found out too late that Carlos's Spanish was not a fluent as he had led us to believe, and his translations were sadly inaccurate. His countrymen had picked up on that and played on it, smiling all the time and saying nothing. I stopped him from waffling on.

'Never mind that Richard, I am waiting to hear the worst and to see if it is salvageable.'

'Sorry. -- Anyway they, the Spaniards, incriminated us just after they had transferred their operation to an off shore company, and then vanished from the face of the earth. The Fraud Squad is in the office now removing all our paperwork for further investigation. We could get up to fourteen years prison sentence each, the maximum for a crime that in our innocence we didn't realise we were committing.'

Knowing this wouldn't go down well with the HMRC (Her Majesty's Revenue & Customs). I asked him what they had said.

'They were not sympathetic and told us that we had set ourselves up as experts without the knowledge to back up our investments, so we deserved the trouble we are in.' Prison? Fourteen years? 'How could you be so stupid' I screamed at him as I was beating him over the head with the Financial Times?

Predictably, I lost my job. The principal couldn't wait to tell me to pack my bags.

'We couldn't possibly have the wife of a criminal teaching in this prestigious school; that would never do' she pronounced. 'The parents would withdraw their children the minute the news got out, and we cannot possibly allow that to happen. Don't even think you will be receiving pay in lieu of notice.' She said as she ushered me out of the back door of the school.

I visited Richard, who was in custody pending his sentence to demand a divorce.

'I don't blame you for thinking that way' he sighed. 'Yes of course you can divorce me. I've been thinking along those lines for quite a while now anyway, as we seem to have totally different ideas as to how we see our future, and I can't imagine where these would come together at any point?' he told me.

I couldn't believe what he had just said. I had no idea he had been contemplating separation. Had I been so wrapped up in myself that I hadn't noticed that he was unhappy? Whilst our marriage wasn't exactly a Romeo and Juliette relationship, I thought it was working.

'I will naturally support the children' he countered.

'What with?' I chided him. 'The money you earn stitching mail bags?' And with that I flounced off. Let him have his divorce, see if I care? Life had taken a very nasty turn for me. Richard was right about my so called friends not wanting to be connected with a criminal element. They dropped me the second they heard of our misfortune. He will have that smug I told you so look on his face when I tell him, because I will have to see him again divorce or not, as he is the father of my children.

Mum couldn't believe it when she heard what had happened as she really loved Richard and thought I was very lucky to have him as a husband. Rhys came in waving the Evening Standard.

'Cor, who would think goody goody Richard would break the law? It's all over the paper tonight.' he cried, practically salivating.

'What will the neighbours think?' Mum snivelled, and you with your degree too. What in God's name that had to do with any of this shit I cannot imagine, but unfortunately what the neighbours thought was very important in suburban life then – maybe it still is -- so I did sympathise with Mum on that score.

Chapter twenty-five
Maggie 1968

I hate living in this country idyll as I don't get on with the locals at all. When we first moved here I made a real effort to fit in by going to every coffee morning, every Bring & Buy and every fund raising gathering I saw advertised, and even watched pony club trials or whatever they are called, to try to meet new friends. I took Michael to a Mothers and Babies group and chatted to people in my usual friendly way, but they all looked at me as if I had come from Mars. I don't blame them in a way, as I thought I had landed on another planet myself. How can life be so different just a few miles outside of London? It's all hunting, fishing and horses round here, all totally alien to me.

There also seems to be a uniform amongst the women of twin sets, frumpy Goray skirts, and pearls. A few brave ones had shortened them slightly, but they were the wrong shape to be miniskirts and looked terrible. My clothes were too bright, too short, and too hippy, so I tried dressing the same way as them hoping they might accept me if I didn't stand out, but that didn't work either. Gerry looked at me sideways frowning, not recognising the girl he had fallen in love with, but said nothing. I tried talking to him about how miserable I was living here and how I didn't fit in but he thought I was making a fuss over nothing, and should make more of an effort to adjust. How could I possibly make more of an effort? I'd tried really hard going to all these boring alien local things to try to fit in to no avail.

I tried telling the women that I wrote a column in the COURIER thinking that might give me a few Brownie points, but that didn't help either, as they only read the Times or the Telegraph, and looked down their stuck up noses at any suggestion of another paper. They were also Tory to a man – or woman -- so I couldn't even join in their debates about the state of the country, as opening my big socialist mouth would have alienated me still further. Poor Sheila, she must be sick to death of hearing me moan on the phone to her. She has been down,-- or maybe it's up?--- a couple of times, but it really is such a difficult place to get to if you haven't got a car and I could see she wasn't comfortable sitting on the Regency chairs, any more than I was. It's like living in a bloody museum set, and I longed for Notting Hill. We had a real mixture of antiques and sixties stuff all together there with lots of colour and it worked like a dream. It was alright for Gerry as he was staying in London overnight more frequently, leaving me stuck out here feeling desperately lonely. I was worried as I had started drinking quite heavily to blot out my miserable life.

I was vaguely friendly with a woman called Imogen. She was a bit more approachable than most the other women I had encountered, but I messed it up with her when I asked her back for a drink one morning.

'What would you like: Gin, whisky, vodka?'

By the look on her face I realised I had committed another social gaffe.

'Decaffeinated coffee would be lovely,' she replied.

I'm not very happy about Michaels progress, as he doesn't seem to be developing like other children of his age .Imogen's little boy is a couple of months younger, but is way ahead of Michael. He responds to his mother -- even answers her back, which I find funny, whereas Michael doesn't say anything at all and just seems locked in a world of his own. Imogen no longer invites us to her home. It was fine when Michael was in his pram, but now he is walking about she made any feeble excuses not to ask us to her house.

'Can we go to your house? Mine is such a mess at the moment, I would be ashamed to take you there' she said last week. Her house wouldn't know what a mess was; it had never been guilty of such a crime. Even her children played tidily. The toys all had a special place and woe betide one of them putting a toy back in the wrong cubby hole. The real reason was she didn't want Michael in her house. He didn't respond to requests – I hesitate to say it --- like normal children do, and takes no notice if you ask him not to touch anything. He has started smashing his toys up and flying into terrible temper tantrums if you cross him in any way. I think there is something very wrong with him. I tried talking to my Mother about my concerns. She, in cloud cuckoo land as always, said I was cruel to criticise him, and as there was nothing wrong with him. Mum doesn't like unpleasantness, and refuses to recognise it when it is right under her nose – I suppose that's the trouble really as he's not under her nose, as she hasn't seen him since the first time they came, so has no idea how oddly he behaves.

I told Gerry that Jen was thinking about taking him to see Dr Hardwick, and I suggested we went with her as I was really worried about his lack of response and the way he doesn't seem to be aware of me, or you, come to that.

'He never makes eye contact; never wants a cuddle; it's not normal, I think he's autistic.' I shouted at him as he didn't seem to be listening.

'Autistic? What in God's name is that? Some new-fangled word for backward children you've picked up from one of those magazines you're always reading?' The conversation was getting heated. Not what I wanted it to do. I just wanted Gerry to take an interest in his son.

'Give him time' he responded, 'He may just be a slow developer.'

'Come off it 'I shouted at him maybe it's not autism and he is not all there.' I could have put that a little more delicately I thought, but I'd said it now, so I couldn't retract. Gerry was furious.

'What a wicked thing to say. He is only two and a half and you are condemning him to the lunatic asylum.'

'Well there have been quite a few loonies in your family tree: your mother told me when we first met'.

'Well she had no right to say such a thing. I'm beginning to wonder what I ever saw in you?' He suddenly threw at me. It took my breath away.

'Judging by all those bottles in the bins, you have become a complete alcoholic.' he accused me. 'I warned you some time ago your drinking was getting out of control, and now it looks as if has. Deal with it' he ordered.

I didn't imagine he would ever sniff around the dustbins. I didn't think he even imagined such things existed he's so ignorant of how households run. Posh boys have nannies and servants running round them to deal with all that basic stuff. Even in Notting Hill we had cleaners three times a week so the reality of how normal people live never concerned him. Then as a parting shot he informed me he had been offered the job as anchor man on News at Ten. I went into orbit.

'You didn't accept it did you?' I yelled at him.

'Yes I did.'

'God knows I see little enough of you as it is, and if you take that job I will hardly see you at all'.

'It would be the same if I were s a foreign correspondent.' he countered.

'No way would it be the same as you wouldn't be in the UK, so nights away were part of the job and therefore acceptable. Spending the week in the London with me stuck out here is not'. I was screaming by now, and all the polish I had acquired over the years vanished, and he must have been reminded that I had come from humble beginnings before marrying him.

'Too bad, I've accepted it now.' he said dismissively and stormed off back to London. I was devastated, and couldn't stop crying. Was my marriage over? Gerry had lived a charmed life having never having to deal with any real pressure, so the only way he could cope with trouble when it hit him, was to run away. I understood that now, and realised an alcoholic wife and a son with problems was just too much for him to handle.

Then, when I thought things could not get any worse, they did. 'Maggie's London' column was dropped. The Editor took the trouble to phone me and tell me personally rather than sacking me by letter, which was often the way these things were done, but I couldn't persuade him to keep me on, even writing on other subjects. I knew not living in London would eventually kill it, and I knew my writing had deteriorated since moving to the country. All the humour had evaporated, because I had lost the ability of seeing the funny side of anything since living in this alien environment. My unhappiness overwhelmed me and I reached for the gin bottle.

Chapter twenty-six
Helen 1971

Life is very strange, and sometimes when you are at your lowest ebb, suddenly, in the most unexpected way everything changes and you are on the up again. I had been turned down for job after job, even one as a cleaner can you believe? The interviewer turned me down flat saying I was overqualified – that was the overstatement of the year. He said he knew I would only use his job as a stop gap until I found a decent one, and he was fed up with people like me. He wanted a girl who was dependable and grateful to have the job. He knew it was only because I was desperate that I had even applied for his lousy job.

Then, as I was walking towards the tube station a young girl, who looked like a model for a cover of one of the magazines for teenagers that have sprung up everywhere, approached me.

'Do you mind telling me how old you are?' she asked.

'I most certainly do' I answered. Who was this child asking me my age? How dare she.

'I'm sorry, I shouldn't have come on to you like that, forgive me. I'm a journalist on a new magazine for older women and . . . '

I'd stopped listening to her diatribe. As she was only about eighteen or nineteen, how could she be a journalist? Ah just a minute! Wasn't Maggie one at the same age?

'Again apologies' she said I'm really making a complete mess of this aren't I? As you probably realise I'm new to this job. Let me make amends to you by buying you a coffee and tell you why I stopped you' she piped up. A gin and tonic would have been preferable but as I had nothing better to do I accepted.

'My name is Cissy she said, and I am acting as a talent scout for models in their mid-thirties to forty for a new magazine aiming for women in that age group that my boss Ruth is about to launch. Are you thirty? 'cos you would be perfect if you are.'

'Regrettably yes, I'm thirty three'. I answered her. 'You said you wanted models. I have never modelled anything in my life, and more to the point, I have never wanted to.'

'Why not, you're beautiful.'

I gasped; nobody had called me beautiful since Richard had been imprisoned. I certainly didn't feel it these days.

'Ruth, the editor, feels all the fashion magazines are aimed at the teens and early twenties with some pretty wild clothes featured, and she feels there is a gap in the market for one especially for the thirty plus group of women who want to look fashionable but not like mutton dressed as lamb.'

'Huh! People like me you mean? Out of work teachers with children to support, who through no fault of their own, can't even afford to buy a glossy magazine.'

'So you're available then. Whoopee! Come along and meet Ruth then' she said whisking me off protesting through the streets behind Selfridges, at that time full of doorway of shabby buildings and we climbed the crumbling stairs to an office on the fourth floor.

'Any luck Cissy?' a voice called out.

'This is Helen. I found her on the way to the tube.'

'Done any modelling before Hel?' 'Not keen on being called Hel, but if they are going to pay me who cares? We went into an office that was so untidy it was difficult to find a chair or table which was not buried under sheaves of paper and sample dresses.

'Definitely not' I replied. 'I'm a teacher by profession.'

'Time for a change then eh? Get 'yer kit off and try these for size. Dressing rooms behind that curtain.' Ruth ordered in a casual way, while she was trying to make sense of a mountain of invoices piled up on a chair. Cissy whispered in my ear laughing quietly at the chaos around us. 'Her dad's got pots of money and indulges his only daughter by buying her anything she wants. She wanted to own a magazine and be the editor, so he bought her this place to edit in.' I tried on some fantastic modern dresses that I have to say looked great on me: a real transformation from my school teacher look. Ruth gasped when she saw me.

'You're hired' she confirmed, 'When can you start?'

It was a case of all hands on deck in order to get the first edition on the streets. Ruth hadn't got a clue what she was doing, but had the good sense to let the odd assortment of staff she had assembled who could do a better job than her get on with it without any interference. I wasn't happy about a longwinded article she had written.

'Ruth, shall I give this article a bit of a rewrite? 'It's a bit ponderous' I told her'

'If you think you can improve it then go ahead love.'

'I've got a first class honours degree in English,' I told her.

'Cor blimey 'luv you've got a job.'

She was a great girl; tall and striking in an exotic Jewish way, good fun and nobody's fool, and I warmed to her immediately. She breathed life into the project inspiring all of us. Billy, her photographer, was the only one there who did know what he was doing, squealed and flounced around the office, taking pictures of the models making us look far more glamorous than we really were. I gasped when I saw the pictures of me. I had always been quite vain about my looks, but he had turned me into a ravishing beauty. It did wonders for my shattered self-esteem. Clothes were borrowed from up and coming young designers who Ruth had persuaded that you were not ready for the graveyard when you reached thirty and to design clothes for them as they wanted to wear modern styles like their younger sisters. These designers paid way over the top for the privilege of appearing in Ruth's as yet untried magazine, such were her powers of persuasion. I thought I am working in Maggie's world and I was in heaven. I had never had so much fun in my life.

Chapter twenty-seven
Maggie 1971

Gerry hardly ever comes home now, and when he does, he can't wait to leave. We never make love on these flying visits and I strongly suspect he is having an affair. I confided my fears to Jennifer, which she dismissed, but I could tell she suspected he was too. I am in despair about Michael He is definitely not developing the way he should. His reaction to me is the most upsetting part of his condition – that is if it is a condition. He avoids any eye contact and refuses to be cuddled. It's as if there is a fog in his brain that acts as a barrier to him understanding emotions, and he is lost in his own little world. He has started to form words instead of that peculiar language he uses to his dinosaur, so I was briefly excited, BUT that was short lived. He didn't use words the way we do -- you know exchanging views, conversation etc.

'Darling, where did you put your shoes?' I would say.

'Darling, where did you put your shoes?' He repeated in a flat monotone voice.

'If you can't find them, we can't go for a walk can we?' I say to him.

'If you can't find...' he continues to repeat my words exactly. I have given up trying to get any normal response from him; it was as if I had given birth to a stranger. Darling Jennifer has decided to take him to see a doctor friend of hers in London for a consultation. Whatever would I do without her?

Jennifer decided to take him to see Dr Hardwick in Harley Street. She didn't ask me to go with her which disappointed me. I would have loved a trip to London. It seems eternity since I was there, and I miss it so much. Maybe she is ashamed of me. I have got so fat with the drinking and none of my clothes fit me anymore and I really look rough. Mum sent me some photographs of Helen, who is working as a model would you believe, and I hate to admit it but she looks fabulous. After seeing those pictures of my arch enemy, looking in the mirror depressed me more than ever as I look ten years older than her. I have got to pull myself together. I really do need help to free myself of this addiction, but I don't seem to have the strength to activate myself to do something about it. Jennifer was disappointed with the outcome of her visit, as all that came out of it was her friend Dr Hardwick, confirmed that Michael was on the Autism spectrum, something which both Jen and I had suspected; having recently read an article in The Lady, – Jen's magazine, not one of mine, I can assure you. Dr Hardwick had told Jennifer there is no known cure for Autism, and as an aside, that when Michael repeats whatever you say to him, is called Echolalia. She said he looked smug when he told her this.

She told me 'I've only known Nigel socially. This is the first—and the last time – I have consulted him professionally' she told me.

'I bet he charged an astronomical price for those words of wisdom.'

'You could say that, but that is not your concern. You are not to worry about that, He also told me Autism had been known to exist since early in the century, however, surprisingly very little research had been carried out into the condition for either a cure, which was thought not to be possible, or at least some chemical intervention to make the child or their carer's lives easier.'

'Maggie, I don't think I realised just how difficult Michael is. I am absolutely worn out after spending a whole day with him. He resists every simple request like sit still or stop yelling doesn't he? Darling girl, I must get you some help. No wonder you have sunk so low, Gerry can jolly well pay for it as he is his son: not that you would know it the way he ignores him. I called in to Notting Hill whilst we were in London hoping to get him to take an interest in Michael, but I am afraid he made some feeble excuse to flee.' I told Jen there was no way I could pay for it anyway as I don't have any money of my own.

'What do you mean? Doesn't Gerry give you an allowance?' I could see she was horrified.

'No, since I got the push from the COURIER I haven't had any income at all.' Did she mean help was finally at hand? Please God let it be then maybe I can beat this depression then I wouldn't drink so much.

Two weeks later

'Where am I? It looks like a hospital, is it? Why am I here? -- I feel like shit. -- Is that Jennifer over there talking to somebody in a white coat? God, have I finally lost it and am in a lunatic asylum? All these thoughts were running through my addled brain as I lay there – then panic set in. I sat up – 'Where's Michael? Who's looking after him?' I remember shouting.

I found out later that Jennifer had tried to telephone me, and when she couldn't get an answer she sensed all was not well and drove straight over to the Big House - (my name for my prison) she found me collapsed on the floor, with Michael running wild and smashing the place up with a baseball bat -- a totally unsuitable present from his father. To restrain him she had to scoop him up and tie him to the banisters with his reins so she could deal with me and call for an ambulance. She had to dash out into the lane to flag it down as the house cannot be seen from the road; but Michael's terrified shrieking could be heard by the ambulance men when they arrived and they thought he was the patient. Jennifer told me herself what happened next.

'I think they were questioning why Michael was tied up, and were looking at me in a very accusative way, ignoring you, so I had to draw their attention to your body on the floor. I had written down your details and told them to go ahead and that I would follow as soon as I had made arrangements for someone to look after Michael...'

'Don't tell me,' I interjected, 'nobody would.'

'I'm afraid you are right, so I had to bring him here and prevail upon the matron to find somewhere and someone in the hospital to care for him temporarily. I've telephoned Gerry and told him to get down here as fast as he can and deal with his responsibilities.' Oh God, he is the last person in the world I want to see. He will probably give me a lecture on my excessive drinking, and he would be justified in doing so. I had sustained a head injury when I collapsed, so the hospital wanted to keep me in for observation, also I was very run down and suffering from exhaustion and the beginnings of malnutrition, which was another reason for them keeping me here.

'Don't you worry about a thing; I'll take care of everything just get better' lovely Jennifer said, and with that she kissed me on my forehead and left, and I felt relieved somebody other than me was dealing with the shambles that my life had become and fell asleep.

Chapter twenty-eight
Helen 1971

Dad is nagging me about leaving the kids with Mum so much – again, so once more I have to search for a nursery for them. Fortunately help was at hand as one of the girls in the office -- no idea what she is employed to do as there are several pretty young girls wandering around looking for work to do to justify their having a job here, and Melanie is one of them. Ruth doesn't seem to have a clue about budgets or running a business. Anyway, Melanie's mother was a registered child minder, and lived near the office and she agreed to take Sophie and Jason, at a price of course .Next I have to find a local school for them. This will be their third move, Frimley Green, Fulham now the West End, all in a matter of a few months. I presume there are schools here somewhere.

However, Ruth was nobody's fool in other ways, and now left most of the writing to me, and the magazine was beginning to gain a regular clientele.

She suddenly looked at me sideways. We were working one day when she suddenly asked if I was Maggie Sutherland's sister by any chance 'cos you look alike. Whatever happened to her? she asked. She was brilliant in her day' she continued. I had reverted to my single name, not wanting to be associated with Richard. Maybe I should have made a name up, as I had no desire to be linked with Maggie either.

'Yes she is but I don't really know where she is as we are not close and I have rather lost touch.' I answered, hoping Ruth wouldn't bring her name up again. Mum's weekly update had become thing of the past, so it was true. I didn't know, nor did I care what she was doing. 'That's sad. I would love to have had a sister to share gossip with.' she said. I ignored her, hoping to bring an end to this conversation. Then, quite by chance, I ran into Gerry. I had forgotten how dashing he was.

'Hello Gerry. What a lovely surprise running into you' I simpered. He looked confused, but at the same time realising he should know who I was. A banal conversation ensued; you know the sort you have with people you haven't got a clue who they are. Then he finally gave in.

'I'm so sorry, frightfully rude of me, but where did we meet?

'I'm Maggie's sister Helen. We met at my grandmother's funeral; Dad insisted the whole family attended.' I was feeling a mixture of embarrassment and pique by now and began to wish I hadn't spoken to him. Because he was on television nearly every night, it was easy for me to recognise him, but he had only met me once at one of the Sutherland family's usual debacles. No wonder he didn't recognise me – he probably didn't want to.

'I am terribly sorry: do forgive me, no wonder you look familiar. Maggie hasn't been well recently, and put on a lot of weight, so the likeness is not so obvious as it once was,' he said by way of an excuse for not knowing who I was.

'Oh dear, I am sorry to hear that'. I said trying to sound if I cared. She's fat is she? Ha ha. 'You are looking fantastic' he said, very different from the way I remember you. Are you working in London now?' The bloody cheek of the man.

'I'm working on a new magazine near here' I told him.

'Oh, competing with Maggie eh? I was about to find a bite to eat, would you care to join me?' I was smarting at his jibe, but I accepted his invitation nevertheless.

We went to a Turkish restaurant at the back of Selfridge's and to cover the fact I hadn't got a clue what to order, I said that I would have the same as him when the waiter took the order.

'How did you get into publishing? I thought you were a teacher, and how is Richard these days?' I ignored the second part of his question and told him how Cissie had found me and whisked me in to meet her boss who offered me a job modelling. I felt his attitude towards me change and he was becoming attracted to me. That would be one up on Mag's if I slept with him I thought, so I went into flirt mode. I hadn't had sex for ages anyway, and feeling spiteful, I decided it was about time I got back into the saddle, so why not with him?

'I never did get to see your Notting Hill flat. Is that where you stay when you are working late?' I asked coyly.

'Yes, perhaps you would like to come over for dinner one evening then you can see it.' 'That would be lovely.' I purred. Gotch yer I thought.

A date was arranged for the following week to visit his beautiful flat, and we flirted our way through a superb meal he had ordered from the chef of his and Maggie's favourite restaurant, and as soon as we had finished our brandies, the tour of the flat began ending up in the bedroom, which was the unspoken intention of .both of us, but the following morning he couldn't get me out of the flat quick enough. It was so embarrassing.

'I hope you won't tell Maggie about last night,' he pleaded with me. What a bastard. How dare he dismiss me like this? He had even called me Maggie when we were making love? I believe his family are Catholic. A boyfriend I had when I was about seventeen had told me deep down in every catholic, even if they had renounced the church, was a nagging feeling that if they had sinned, they would eventually be punished for it. Maybe that was why he was being such a shit? His phone rang.

'Hi mum, what's up?'

He went very pale. 'OK I'll be there as soon as possible' and hung up.

'Maggie's been taken to hospital. Mum found here collapsed in the hall of our house. I must go. Here are the keys; please lock up and put them through the letterbox as you leave.

My God, I think he still loves her. 'Thanks Bye' and off he went leaving me feeling used and dirty.

How dare he treat me in such a dismissive way? I'll get my revenge eventually. I'm in no hurry.

Chapter twenty-nine
Maggie 1971

My alcoholic poisoning and subsequent collapse frightened the life out of me. I could have died. This came as a big shock to me because I thought that's what I wanted to do, but NO --. I wanted to LIVE and be me again -- to sort out my life, and what's more, change it. I saw Jennifer, dear loyal loving Jennifer, making her way across the ward. I told her what I had been thinking.

'Darling, I know how unhappy and depressed you are, and I hope what I have arranged will meet with your approval. I have engaged a nurse, Pat Ryan, whose sister suffered from autism -- or rather her family suffered; -- the sister was oblivious to the trouble she caused, so Pat is not only medically trained but she understands Michael's problems. She has moved into the house already to care for him. I'm sure you will like her and she will also be company for you, instead of you having to be on your own so much. I have also arranged for you to meet Dr Myra Schofield who is a therapist and can help you with your addiction and depression. I do hope you will forgive me for interfering, and you must feel free to reject anything I have arranged for you.'

Forgive her? I could have kissed her there and then, and burst into tears. Tears were never far away, which was another part of me I wanted to stop. I used to be a feisty bird, and would stand my ground, not burst into tears every five minutes. Then I saw Gerry heading my way.

I'll go now, but I will be back this afternoon.' Jennifer said glaring at Gerry. I heard her whisper to him a lot of this is your fault you know, we'll talk later.

I didn't know what to say to him and then, HE was the one who burst into tears. I found myself embarrassed by them, which was too cruel, as why shouldn't a man show his emotions. He kept apologising almost grovelling, begging me to forgive him. Forgive him for what? It wasn't his fault that I couldn't cope with the life he offered me. I realised. I wanted him to go. This wasn't the man I had loved so deeply, any more than I was the girl he had met and married. Too much water had flowed under the bridge for us to reconcile our differences. We both thought we had been let down by the other one, but really we should never have got together in the first place. After he left it was my turn to burst into tears, AGAIN and I sobbed inconsolably for an hour, then much to my surprise, it had been cathartic moment, and I felt quite cheerful afterwards.

Chapter thirty
Helen 1972

I suppose it was inevitable; the magazine had been so badly run as none of us really knew what we were doing, and although the circulation was picking up quite nicely, it was losing so much money that Ruth's indulgent father decided to pull the plug on it. She reacted as if her child had died, and she sobbed for days. She even buried a few copies in her garden with a headstone commemorating its life, death, and subsequent murder by her father. A bit bizarre I thought.

Now I was out of work again. 'Don't lose touch Ruth cried out as I left the building. I loved that job. I might have guessed it was too good to be true, and I was almost as upset as Ruth about its demise. I eventually found a teaching job in a struggling school in East London. I think the only reason I got it was because the Head had been losing staff on a weekly basis because of the appalling behaviour of the pupils so he would have taken anyone who applied. A bit insulting really: he's lucky to have me with my qualifications. I hated every minute I worked there.

Then out of the blue Ruth got in touch and suggested we met up for a drink or a meal. Mum agreed to have the kids for the night so I was able to meet her. During the course of the evening she regaled me with a madcap scheme she had dreamt up where the clients cooked their own food at their table.

'But I thought the whole idea of going out to a restaurant was so you didn't have to cook? Is your dad going to back you again?' I asked her thinking the idea was ludicrous.

'No darling, sadly not, he doesn't trust me to give him a return on his money, mean old thing; he'll be sorry when I make a killing with the idea one day. It'll be a riot you'll see.' One drink led to another, and yet another until we were both so drunk we had to hold each other up as we walked – or rather staggered back to Ruth's enormous flat giggling like idiots. No taxi would take us. I think the drivers had more respect for the interior of their cabs to let two drunken women inside them. Back in the flat we made an abortive attempt at making omelettes, but the eggs seemed to prefer to drop on the floor than in the pan, so giggling like silly school girls we gave up that idea and phoned for a Chinese instead and left the eggy mess to be cleared up in the morning.

'I think its bed time don't you darling?' Ruth slurred and guide me to a huge king sized bed which she obviously intended us to share.

'I fancied you like mad the first time I saw you Hel. Do you feel the same, as I've caught you looking at me that way once or twice?' I blushed; this was not what I had anticipated. However, she was right. I knew she was a lesbian and I had often looked at her and wondered what it would be like to go to bed with a woman. Oh well I thought what the hell, I will never know what I may have missed if I don't try will I? I've been so busy being respectable, and look where that got me – nowhere, so here goes.

Chapter thirty-one
Maggie 1971

The depression I had lived with for so long seemed to have lifted slightly after I returned from hospital. It was Pat Ryan, the nurse Jennifer had employed to help me look after Michael, who I had to thank for that. We got on from day one, and her cheerful persona brought a ray of sunshine into the house. I used to be a sociable and gregarious person and apart from visits from Jennifer, I hardly ever saw a soul and I could go all day without speaking to anyone... anyone that is apart from Michael, and bless him, that's not exactly stimulating. He was talking a lot more these days, but autistic kids go on and on about their interest – Michael's is trains. His walls are covered with pictures of trains, of stations and he will recite timetables ad infinitum. Not exactly stimulating. I had long ago given up the idea of having any sort of conversation with Mrs Gregory, the cleaner who comes in a couple of days a week. From day one she treated me as an interloper into the Macintyre family, and in her view definitely not good enough for Master Gerry, and she only ever addresses me formally.

'Is there anything special Madam requires of me today?'

'Just the usual.' I would reply and that was the sum total of our exchange of words. She gives me the creeps and I avoid her whenever she is around.

Pat had a deep understanding of all aspects of the autism spectrum as her sister Teresa had suffered from it – or rather Teresa didn't -- but everyone around her was affected by her behaviour. Pat learned all she could about the syndrome by reading every paper published and questioned any doctor willing to enlighten her further. Autism had been recognised as a syndrome from the beginning of the twentieth century, but very little research had been undertaken to understand the condition more over the intervening years. Children affected were often described as odd or strange and those more severely affected and many of them were hidden away in institutions, but Pat was not going to let that happen to Michael. She spoke to my doctor about a drug that had helped one of her previous patients and he prescribed it for Michael. It has definitely made a difference to his general behaviour. Pat feels with the right help, he could possibly live a relatively normal life. However, she told me he would never love me the way a child loves his mother, as he didn't understand emotions, and never would, and I will have to learn to deal with that. Her words made me feel very sad.

Jennifer has arranged for me to see a therapist, Dr Myra Schofield to help me deal with my alcoholism and depression. I really didn't want to go down that path, but I could hardly refuse as she had gone to so much trouble for me.

'It's very beautiful round here isn't it? Pat remarked.

'I suppose it is' I replied.

Shamefully I had hardly noticed my surroundings since I had lived here, but country views would never be my choice of scenery. I liked towns and buildings, love architecture and didn't know what to focus the camera on with all that green stuff.

'I must ask mum to bring my camera when she comes to visit next time.' Pat said. A camera? – mm. Maybe I should fish mine out of wherever they are. I've got several, so I could easily give Pat one of mine. She was thrilled when I did as it was a much better model than the one she'd left with her mum.

'Maybe we could go on a photographic sortie together?' I ventured. She could hardly refuse I thought seeing as I had given her the camera. Jennifer called round and volunteered to look after Michael and sent us out there and then. Nature needed colour photography and I had only ever worked in black and white, necessary at that time for reproduction in newspapers. I took shots of people having fun, girls in the great new fashions that were around, the new buildings that were replacing the old slums and bombed houses that were still to be found in parts of London, all far more dramatic in black and white.

Pat was excited and snapped away merrily, taking shots of scenes that didn't look the slightest bit interesting to me. My work was awful compared to hers. 'Can't have that can I? I'm supposed to be the professional. But I soon learnt and even started to appreciate my surroundings. I was ashamed of myself for never having taken any notice of the area where I lived when it was so beautiful.

I had been attending A A meetings (Alcoholics Anonymous) for a couple of months which had been deeply depressing at first but now I began to be curious as to why people became alcoholic, whilst others, who drank just as heavily, didn't. I found myself talking to my fellow 'alkies' as if I was interviewing them for an article. They didn't seem to mind which surprised me. I asked Alan, one of the members of the group if he would mind if I took notes while we were talking.

'Why would you want to do that?' he asked me in a hostile voice.

'Well, I told him; before the drinking got out of hand I was a journalist.'

He sounded hurt. 'I thought I was a mate, not a case study' he said.

'Oh Alan I'm so sorry, you are a mate. You have helped me so much just by listening to me; I really didn't mean to offend you.' I pleaded with him. He relaxed

'Course you can love, only don't use my name for God's sake, or I will never work again.'

'Why, what was your job?'

'It **is** my job; I **am** still working. It's been touch and go once or twice, but you must know how devious we drunks can be when it's necessary, and I've managed to hang in there.' I laughed; remembering one or two near misses at the COURIER. Sliding off my chair was one that needed some explaining to my editor.

Frank, the ex-addict leader of the group was apprehensive about members thinking I was being intrusive. However, I think I often got more out of the guys because I was a girl than he did with all his experience. The group was eighty-five percent male, and there was always pride and one-up-manship to contend with in any male dominated group, so I think my face to face method of questioning helped in a different way than in group discussions. I realised I was definitely beginning to shake off the depression; otherwise I would never have attempted to talk to people the way I was doing at the moment. Oh please God let it be. I do so want to be me again.

'Maybe they see me as a challenge?' Frank speculated looking a bit upset.

I reassured him saying it was a fact of life that men always confided in women as they didn't want to lose face with other men. They didn't have this problem with women and I told him he was fantastic with the group, which was true. He cheered up then.

'Let's try it, but the slightest sign of a problem and you stop. OK?' I was so deep in my own thoughts I had to shake myself and take in what Frank was saying, but whatever it was it culminated in him agreeing to me carrying on, BUT to make sure I let him know what I had gleaned from my interviews.

After a while I felt confident enough to write a paper on addiction and showed it to Frank. He interspersed it with his own views and ideas between my paragraphs and we were delighted with the result.

'Shall we publish it?' he asked. 'Sorry, no it's too soon for me to put my name to an article at the moment. I wasn't ready for that yet. A few weeks later I realised I was not being fair to Frank by not wanting to publish. It would only be in only a medical paper or something like that. I didn't know how people like Frank got their information updates, but I imagine it is through trade papers: so I told him to go ahead if he wanted to: it was just a report on how we had worked together to help the addicts. It did get published in one of the papers he received from time to time. He was over the moon.

Myra asked me to come to her practise in Wigmore Street instead of her coming to see me in my home. My home? Wow! That's the first time I've ever called the Big House that.

I was excited by the idea of going to London for the first time in nearly four years, but nervous at the same time. Good old Jennifer came to the rescue again.

'How about I come on the train with you and leave you near Myra's then pick you up later, when you're ready. Then we can go to somewhere wildly expensive for lunch?' So that's what we did. The minute we arrived in London, I felt the old excitement I always felt just by being in there – silly I know, but that's how London always affected me. It gave me a huge lift, and I knew exactly what I wanted to do.

'Myra, I want to move back to London as soon as possible' I gabbled. 'Do you think I will be able to cope?' Please don't say no I thought. She took her time before she answered.

'I don't see why not BUT remember you are not cured. There is no cure for either depression or addiction, so you always have to be aware of them creeping up on you again. But I am here, and if you continue to see me for a while when you first return, I am sure you will be fine.' I couldn't wait to tell Jen my decision.

Chapter thirty-two
Helen 1971

When Ruth and I were out for a drink one night, I told her just how much I hated living with Mum and Dad, when she surprised me.

'Why don't you move in with me darling, there's plenty of room in my place as you know.'

I was taken aback. That's very sweet of you I responded, but haven't you forgotten, I've got two kids.'

'I meant all of you. I love kids and always wanted them, but it was not to be.'

I was confused. How do lesbians get pregnant? I asked her somewhat naively.

The same way you do darling, a bloke has to do his stuff. It's the only way – apart from the turkey baster of course.' Embarrassed I decided not to pursue this conversation. I wasn't too sure about this lesbian thing but hey ho, but I hadn't got much else going for me at present, so let's give it a go, and I jumped at the chance of moving into the fabulous flat her father had bought her. I met the kids from school and told them we were on the move again.

'Oh no Mum, not again' they chorused.

'Oh yes, and I don't want any complaining from the pair of you.' I countered.

'But Mum that will be four different schools we will have been to in four years.' Oh dear, she's right – too bad, were moving I told them.

'Blame your Dad darling. He's the one who put us in this mess.' Richard had been lucky, he was only given five years, so with good behaviour he would be out in half that time; such are the peculiarities of the English judicial system. His friend Carlos had been given ten years, as the judge or magistrate whatever he was called, saw him as the guilty one who had misled his colleagues into breaking the law. Nonsense of course, Richard was as guilty as hell. He should have checked the Spanish Bank more carefully instead of taking Carlos's word for its credibility.

I wonder if there would be a chance of reconciliation when Richard gets out of prison. It won't be long now. We had never got around to finalising the divorce, so technically we are still married. I have lived such a rackety life since his incarceration. Not me at all: I like being married: I like the stability and status it gives you. Mind you, I don't suppose I will get much of either of those with an ex con husband. Anyway I might meet another man one day; one who is brave enough to take on another man's children. You never know. I don't suppose Ruth will be best pleased if we do get back together, but I have never seen my relationship with a woman as a permanent situation. I like men too much, but this time, it's got to be the right one, and he has to be solvent.

'Dad, can you help me move my stuff? I called out to him I'm moving in with Ruth,'

'Whose Ruth, what about the kids? But he wasn't that worried and couldn't wait to get the cases out of the loft

'You two get a move on, pack up your bits and pieces' I called out to my kids, as 'I want to be in our new home tonight'

Mum has forwarded a letter from Richard addressed to me. I suppose he thought we were still living with my parents. Anyway, he wants me to meet him when he is released next week. I suppose I owe him that so I wrote to him to say that I would. I didn't want to be recognised, so disguised myself with a wig, and heavy makeup, not something I usually wear, and waited at the gates for him. There were some awful women waiting for their men and they tried to engage me in conversation. I would have none of that. What on earth would I have in common with them? Ah yes. We were all married to criminals. I hate Richard for putting me in this humiliating position? He came through the gates and walked straight past me. Then I remembered my disguise and chased after him.

'Sorry, I didn't recognise you.' he remarked, looking at me very oddly.

'That was the idea; I didn't want anyone to recognise me.'

'Why, do you frequent this part of London now? You have come down in the world.' He sneared. Bastard!

'Where are you living now? You haven't given me your new address. By the way, that wig couldn't look more false if it tried. I want to see the kids tomorrow' he demanded. .Something you seem to have forgotten is **we** have two children, and as their father I need to know where they live?' Oh my God, he thinks he's going to stay with us. There's no way I'm having that. He might guess what my relationship with Ruth is and then there would be no chance of reconciliation – if that's what I want?

-- Do I really want that? No I don't think so. My life is such shit, I'm just clutching at straws. Guessing part of what I was thinking he said

'You needn't worry; I won't prevail on your good nature for somewhere to stay,' he sneared, 'I've been given an address by a prisoner's rehabilitation group, so I have somewhere to go. Also I've been given enough money for a taxi as well, so you won't have to pay for one. Give me your phone number, or is that on MI5s not to be revealed list?' His words were laden with sarcasm. Why does he feel it necessary to be so nasty? I came to meet him didn't I?

Chapter thirty-three
Maggie 1971

The following day after my consultation with Myra, I telephoned Jennifer to see if she was free. Between her commitments as Chair of the local Conservatives, the Conservation committee, the European Movement and the countless other charities she supports she wasn't always readily available. Good, she's in.

'Jen, I'm on my way over, I need to talk to you. It's important and I need your approval.' I yelled up the stairs to Pat and told her I was going out, and jumped into my car. Half way to Jennifer's I realised I hadn't driven for months – Was I up to it? Of course I was and I found myself grinning from ear to ear. I'm me again. Hurrah!

We sat down in Jens luxurious drawing room and I was gabbling with excitement, trying to tell her about my decision to return to London.

'Slow down, I can't follow what you are saying' she laughed. 'And you don't need my approval as whatever you decide to do I will always support you.

'I want to move back to London as quickly as possible. I felt like me again yesterday. I can't explain it, but I belong there, and I realise I should never have left. It was wrong of me to marry Gerry much as I loved him. We are from different worlds and the marriage was never going to work.' A shadow passed across Jennifer's face and she looked so sad.

'I realise now Gerry and I made a big mistake uprooting you and bringing you here to live with the pony club set. It's a place totally alien to you and I am deeply sorry for encouraging the move.' I was upset that she was blaming herself for my breakdown.

'Oh Jennifer, please don't blame yourself' I told her '.It's my fault for not making a bit more of an effort to fit in. I gave up too quickly. You have been a wonderful friend to me from the day we met. I will always be eternally grateful for that and I will love you forever, so please don't beat yourself up over my inadequacies.' Jennifer had tears in her eyes. I don't think her children ever say I love you to her, although I have no doubt they do, but the schools they went to were all of the stiff upper lip variety and they were taught not to show their emotions openly. I told her of my intention of asking Gerry for a divorce although I still I love him, but it was the only way forward for both of us. I have long suspected Gerry has been having an affair, and he may want to take it a step further.

'Surely not?' she said.

'Face the facts Jen: he hardly ever comes here these days, not that I blame him the way I have been, and he never sleeps with me when he is here and he can't wait to get away. Maybe when I move back to London he might overcome his dislike, or shame, or whatever it is he feels about Michael, and he might just come and see him sometimes. Who knows?' I carried on telling her I would need Gerry's help to buy a flat as I no longer have any money of my own, but hopefully I will be earning again so I only need money for Michael's care.'

'You will qualify for a lot more than that my dear, and I will see to it that you get it. I hadn't realised Gerry had not been giving you any money for yourself. I am absolutely disgusted with him.' Jennifer responded.

Six months later

Nearly four years had passed since my move to the country, and now I finally felt strong enough to think about working again. I thought about the job Alex McDonald had offered me all that time ago, and wondered if he had any vacancies in his company, so I sent him the articles I had written about alcoholism and autism as possible subjects for documentary films – that's if he was still making films on social problems. The minute he received them he was on the phone to me.

'Come and see me ASAP.' he invited. I was thrilled, but I told him

'I'm not sure I was up to that yet, as I've been ill recently, and I'm still a bit shaky.

'Oh, is that why you have dropped off the radar for so long. I wondered where you had got to. Supposing I send a car for you, will that help?'

'Do you mind? I'm moving back to London soon, but at the moment I live out in the Wild Wood.' He laughed,

'Give me your address and I'll tell the driver to avoid the weasels and stoats on the way'. I grinned, a guy with a sense of humour.

'That will be great, and then I won't have to do battle with trains and the tube which was worrying me after all this time away from the smoke. Thank you.' I was shaking with excitement, and couldn't wait to see him.

My meeting with Alex was more like a reunion of old friends than a possible interview for a job. We had only met a couple of times before, but I felt as if I had known him for years, and we talked and talked and talked. Then I disgraced myself. I had returned to my world, and was so overwhelmed with joy and excitement, that I burst into tears.

'Whatever is wrong sweetie? Have I upset you in any way?'

'No I told him in fact quite the contrary. It's the first time in what seems like years that I have felt truly happy. Thank you so much Alex.'

He gave me a big hug and kissed me on the lips, which I surprised myself by returning.

'Come back to my place' he begged me.

'Is that part of your interviewing technique?' I laughed feeling embarrassed at my response to his kiss.

'Maggie, I'm so sorry. I don't know what came over me.'

'Blame me' I told him. 'It's my fault for encouraging you. I am so happy at the idea of working again, and so hyped up that these feelings could end up with us making a big mistake, and I don't think that would be a good idea do you?

'You are probably right he agreed, but phone me the minute you move back to London, and we will talk about how I can help you job wise'. I looked at him -- he really was rather dishy. He was over six foot, thick sandy coloured hair --- Cut that out Maggie I told myself. 'Can't be doing with any of that. Look what happened the last time I slept with my boss.

Gerry had reluctantly agreed to a divorce once he realised there was no way back for us, and he gave me – with a certain amount of prodding from his mother – a very generous settlement. Not that it was going to affect his pocket much, as the house in Fulham I was given came from the Macintyre's property portfolio. He did have to make provision for Michael's future though, and he agreed to pay me a tidy sum each month which once I start earning again I will cancel. Not that I told him that, but it's what I have decided to do.

Leaving day finally arrived. I journeyed up to London with the moving van two days before Pat and Michael so I was able to indulge myself in my new home and wander about from room to room claiming them as my own before anyone else was in the house. Oh joy! It had six bedrooms so Pat, who had agreed to move to London with me, could have a bedroom, a bathroom, and a sitting room of her own, and after choosing a bedroom for me and one for Michael, I will still have two guest rooms left.

I don't know who was most thrilled when Pat agreed to move, her or me. She had become a good friend and invaluable to me. She had done wonders for Michael getting him to talk and he had become so much easier to live with now. She had already researched a school for him which had received some excellent reports on their methods of treating autistic kids. I had enrolled him there before we moved to make sure of a place. Pat had already signed herself up for a course on child care, which included lectures on the latest findings on autism.

I called Mum and Dad to give them my new address and phone number, and left a message on their answer phone. 'Before Pat, Michael and Jen arrived, I claimed a ME moment and flopped onto my new bright red sofa in my newly decorated house where I had chosen the colour scheme and everything else in it, and toasted my new life with a glass of orange juice. It would have been better with a glass of Pinot Grigio, but that can never ever happen again.

'God bless this house and all who live in it.' I yelled at the top of my voice. 'May we be happy, productive and joyful ... then the phone interrupted me. Bugger, I was enjoying myself. My moment of indulgence was over. It was Dad.

'Come quickly, your Mother has been taken into hospital. She's got pneumonia and is in a bad way.' Oh God, I hope that's not going to be the start of more bad things in my new life.

Rhys was at Mums bedside when I arrived at St Stephens. I didn't recognise him at first he looked so smart.

'Hi Mags Long time no see.'

'What are you up to these days?'

Because I had been so wrapped up in my own little world for so long – depression makes you very selfish – I hadn't phoned home for months so I had no idea where he worked, or even if he did.

'I'm the manager of a local super market. Got promoted last week didn't I? Where did you get that posh voice from? It weren't from round ere.' Posh voice? What's he talking about? But I suppose being with Gerry and his mother for so long, their speech patterns must have rubbed off on me without me realising it. Better revert speaking to Mum and Dad or they will think I have got above myself and would never do: only Helen is allowed to speak differently in Mum's way of thinking *because she has a degree.* Stop it -- I'm being pathetic. Bloody Helen. She always has that effect on me.

'Hello Mum, how are you?'

Rhys chastised me, 'Silly cow, how do you think she is? She 'aint come in 'ere for an 'oliday.' Mum gave me a weak smile, then Helen arrived and her smile broadened. Nothing ever changes. We stared at each other not quite knowing how to react. It had been four years since Granny's funeral, which was the last time we had seen each other.

'How are you? We said in unison, and we both smiled at each other. 'Pity meeting up again in these circumstances isn't it?' Helen said. Was she being friendly? Gritting my teeth I told her I was about to move back to London and suggested we meet up for lunch soon, regretting it as soon as I opened my mouth.

'Lovely idea' Helen responded, but I couldn't discern if she was enthusiastic or not. There was a soft bleat from Mums bed,

'Why are you all here? Am I dying?'

'No Mum.'

'Course not –'

'No way'

Dad appeared. He had been speaking to the Doctors and Rene had been pronounced out of danger, and would probably be able to return home in a few days.

'That doesn't mean you lot can disappear. You can all come back to the house and stay the night,' he ordered. We all made feeble excuses why we couldn't stay.

'I've got to pick up the kids.'

'Michael and Jennifer are arriving tomorrow.'

'It's my first day as manager.'

But realising he had issued an order; we all reverted to childhood and complied meekly to our father's command. Dad ordered Pizzas all round. Wow, foreign food being allowed into the family home? Amazing! Things have changed. He didn't ask any of us for our preference so it was

Margaritas all round or go without. He then organised the sleeping arrangements and allocated Helen and me our old room, only it was Rhys's now and he was not best pleased. Being in our old bedroom disturbed us somewhat. The walls were covered with Rhys trash, naked ladies, formula one cars and footballers.

'Surely he's a bit old for this stuff.' I commented.

'I've lived here on and off recently, so I have seen it before.'

'All well with you and Richard?'

'All well with you and Gerry?'

We asked each other in unison again, and we burst out laughing, finally relaxing with each other a little.

'No, we are getting a divorce.'

'No, we are getting a divorce, again in unison.

'This is getting creepy.' Helen rejoined. That's the sort of thing twins are supposed to do and we never did. It was pathetic the way we used to fight. There really isn't any reason to carry on with all that petty jealousy any longer – if that's what it was.' Helen questioned. We decide to meet soon, and have a meal together. That'll please Mum, even if we're apprehensive about the idea.

Chapter thirty-four
Helen 1970

I cannot believe that the four of us are sitting round the family table eating pizza, enjoying each other's company. If only it had always been like this.

Dad is positively purring at the three of us getting on. Maggie and I had never really taken much notice of Rhys — too busy sniping at each other I suppose, but listening to his story of how he lost his job in Carnaby Street had the three of us laughing together because he kept saying *'It weren't my fault'* when it clearly was. He was telling us how he came to leave home in the first place; naturally I knew, as it was my kids who were cited as the reason if I recall.

'I thought, I'm living in London but why was it not *swinging* which is what your column Maggie, and all the magazines I read said it was, and I wanted some of the action. Also Helen, your screaming brats were keeping me awake at night, so

I decided to leave 'ome.' I couldn't let him get away with that one, and had a go at him.

'Stop that,' Dad ordered, and we did – much to both of us amazement.

'I thought you would put me up for a couple of days Mag's until I found a job, but you shoved me out of the way so nobody in your 'ouse could see me. What was that all about?'

'We were moving to the country, so I couldn't put you up. But - excuse me -, you said until you got a job. Seeing as you had never made any serious attempt at finding a job since leaving school, I could see that couple of days stretching on for months with you draped all over the sofa watching tele' all day and not making any attempt to find a job. No thanks matey.' Maggie told him.

'Anyway I got a job straight away, so there. You were all wrong weren't yer. I walked into this guy's shop in Carnaby Street, and he took me on immediately. He said I was the right person to model his clothes as well as sell them. I thought the clothes were a bit poncey, but who was I to argue with him if he was going to pay me for looking like a prat. I couldn't believe the prices he charged for his clobber. My first sale was a suit that I had to keep looking at the ticket to make sure I'd got it right. Three hundred and forty five quid, can you believe? The customer didn't bat an eyelid and just peeled the cash off from a huge roll. I'd never seen so much money in my life.' Thinking about the problems of finding anything affordable to rent in London I asked him where he lived.

'I shared a house in Paddington with six other blokes and a girl who worked at Geezers 'Was she your girlfriend?' I chipped in.

'Nah! She was too posh for me. All her boy friends were called Tristan, Sebastian or Julian and soppy names like that.'

'Perhaps she wasn't so much that she was too posh for you; maybe **you** were too rough for her.' I interjected. Maggie and Dad laughed. Rhys was offended.

'Come on, tell us how you got the push' I encouraged him.

'*It weren't my fault.*' Marco made me the manager before I was ready for it didn't he? The horrible sales staff wouldn't do what I told them, said I was bossy and they all left. I was stuck on my own trying to dress the window, serve the customers and pick up the clothes they just drop on the floor when Marco walked in. Sacked me on the spot didn't he the bastard? Told me he wouldn't give me the money I'd already earned saying that would pay for some of the clobber that had probably been nicked in the chaos.' Visualising the whole debacle all three of us were laughing our heads off.

'You can laugh, *it weren't my fault'*, he repeated – again.

'I couldn't get another job in Carnaby Street as the news spread that Marco had sacked me and before I had even walked out of the door, about four buggers were there applying for my job. Stop laughing you lot, it wasn't funny, I was hurt and upset he said, putting on a tragic face to prove it. I went round Kensington looking for work, thinking they wouldn't know about me getting the push, but believe it or not they did. Gawd knows 'ow, so I 'ad to come home didn't I? Dad had a go at me then saying I'd moved back to let Mum wait on me hand and foot.'

'You wouldn't have even bothered to look for a job until I gave you that ultimatum.' Dad piped up. 'I told 'im, I'll give you three weeks to get one or you're out on your ear. Isn't that right son? Best thing I ever did, that's when you got a job in the super market wasn't it? You wouldn't have bothered otherwise.'

'Anyway, I've been working in the supermarket for a couple of years now and they've offered me the manager's job, so I 'aint done too badly 'ave I? 'Rhys questioned.

I gave him some advice telling him to remember the lessons of his first job. Make a work plan, and tell you're' staff nicely but firmly what you want them to do and why, and **don't** boss them about.' He didn't appreciate it, and glared at me. Then Maggie chipped in.

'Helen's right you know and I hope you're paying Mum and Dad for your keep, and why are you still living at home anyway? You are thirty years old for God's sake. Its time you had a place of your own.'

'Course I'm paying 'em' he snapped' and you needn't tell me what to do Helen. You 'aint made a great success of your life 'ave you?' I was furious. How dare he talk to me like that?

The hospital phoned the following morning and said Mum could come home by the end of the week, so we said our goodbyes and went our separate ways, promising not to leave it so long before we all met up again. I returned home and asked Ruby if I could have one of the spare rooms as a sitting room so I could have my family round sometimes.

'Do you mean so you can leave my bed?'

'No not at all.' I promised her, 'it's only so I can have somewhere of my own to go to sometimes.' 'Not sure if she believed me. Ruby's not stupid but she gave me another room.

Chapter thirty-five
Maggie 1971

On my first day in the office of Alex McDonalds Productions. I felt as nervous as I had on my first day at the COURIER, but I needn't have worried. I got a round of applause from the staff as I walked in, and I had to stop myself from crying with relief and pleasure.

(I really am going to conquer this crying business and toughen up a bit) I found I was on the selection committee where discussions as to what our next production was to be took place. Alex had sounded out the BBC and ITV to see if there would be any interest in a series of four films on subjects such as Autism, Alcoholism, Mental Health issues and Child Poverty.

The BBC had told him 'They're not a load of laughs Alex. Auntie is heavily into laughs at the moment mate, but you know how things work around here. Leave it for a few months eh?' ITV had pronounced the project 'Much too serious for our audience.'

Tim Harcourt, the production manager stated he was not sure this idea is going to set the Thames on fire at this moment in time. Let's stick to the plight of the whales for our next biggie.' It was agreed unanimously to put the idea on the back burner for a while. I found out the company made lots of advertising films for commercial companies as well as the documentaries.

'They are the bread and butter that allow us to make our exposure films,' Alex told me. The guy in charge of the research team has suggested I join him on the boat that will follow the whales on their migration along the North American coastline to the Arctic, and Alex is going to send me to Japan with an investigative team to report on the reluctance of the Japanese people to stop the carnage of these wonderful creatures in the name of research. What research? They eat them. Darling Pat was happy to be in sole charge of Michael whilst I was away, and Jennifer said she would come down to London and give Pat a break now and again, so off I went. Heaven!

The documentary proved to be a big success, raising awareness of the butchering of these highly intelligent animals, and the risk that they could become extinct if some control was not introduced. What a privilege it was to be involved in making the film. I loved every minute of it, even when I was freezing to death on the deck of the boat in the Arctic and throwing up. I was bruised and battered and getting tossed about the ship when riding high on the Atlantic breakers, but I didn't care. It was exhilarating and I felt our work would make a difference to the world's attitude to these beautiful intelligent creatures. I became a life time member of the Save the Whales protest group. I hadn't given tem a thought before I was involved in the making of our film, and felt ashamed that I hadn't. Maybe I should enrol for an Open University course. Maggie's London was journalism on a trivial level, but I am in with the big boys now and need to up my game.

Chapter thirty-six
Helen 1971

'Ruth, I can't believe it. Richard has served divorce papers on me sighting. Irreconcilable differences. What a cheek'. I yelled up the stairs.

'I thought that was what you wanted.'

'Yeah, but I want it to be my decision if and when we divorce.'

'Bit of a selfish cow aren't you darling, always wanting things your way.'

She said this in a jocular way, but I think she meant it.

'No I'm not I retorted.'

'Then how about you cough up something towards the housekeeping now and again sweetness? Your kids are super, and I love then to bits, BUT they have enormous appetites, and although I am delighted to have you all living in my pad, I hadn't reckoned on financing the entire family. You do have a job after all.' Oh dear, I've upset her. That won't do, I'm on to a good thing here so I'd better come to some sort of financial arrangement with her.

'Sorry darling I am naughty aren't I?' I purred. 'How much shall I pay you a week?' She gave me a quizzical look. 'Never mind about the rent, but at least something towards the food and heating costs would help. How does that grab you?' I think I have come out with that very well, so I will pay up with a smile.

'I will make a standing order payable to you darling. And I am sorry for being so thoughtless'. She likes me calling her darling. It embarrasses me, but I need to keep in with her. If I had my own place with the kids it would cost me ten times that amount.

'Mum, Auntie Maggie's documentary about the whales is on tonight. Can we watch it?' Sophie asked. How do you know she's in it?' I asked her. 'There's a picture of her in the Radio Times' Ruth said, showing the offending picture to me. 'What have they put a picture of her in the bloody paper for? She's not the producer or the camera man. What could I say other than yes? Just when I am trying not to be so negative about my feelings for Maggie, but when she pops up in the limelight it makes me feel resentful all over again. 'Why don't you swallow your pride and phone her to congratulate her on her involvement in such an excellent programme?' Ruth asked me. 'I bet she could help you get a job you enjoy. Show her some of the articles you wrote for *THE GO GETTER* were really good. I gritted my teeth. Ruth was right, but could I bring myself to ask her for help? Don't think so.

Then, out of the blue Maggie phoned me. We were so unused to talking on the phone, or any other way come to that, so we both gabbled, frightened there might be a gap in the conversation. Anyway she phoned to ask me out to lunch and suggested we met at Judges. Because my social life had disappeared down a big black hole, I wasn't up to date with the names of fashionable restaurants, but discovered from Ruth that this was the in place at the moment. Shit! How am I going to afford my share?

Chapter thirty-seven
Maggie and Helen 1971

Maggie

I've just returned home after spending the weekend with Jennifer, and I'm feeling peaceful and happy having enjoyed myself so much, so, feeling magnanimous I decided to ring Helen and ask her to meet me for lunch. Big mistake: I had no idea how to speak to her after all this time, and realised neither of us had anything in common, so what on earth were we going to talk about over lunch. We had broken the ice a bit when Dad made us share our old bedroom when Mum was in hospital, but I don't think we really had any idea of how either of us had been living over the past few years.

'Hi Helen. Fancy meeting up for lunch next week?' I said, my voice sounding too high and over enthusiastic'.

'Oh – I am not sure. Let me check my diary' she replied. She hasn't got a bloody diary I bet. She is just trying to sound as it she has a riotous social life.

'I can squeeze you in Wednesday or Thursday', she replied in a condescending way. 'Wish I hadn't asked. 'OK Wednesday suits me: I'll book. Meet you at one o'clock at Judges. Do you know where it is?' Did she just gulp? It's fiendishly expensive and I know she doesn't have much of an income on a teacher's pay, so I really should have told her it was my treat.

'Hi, been waiting long'? I asked her.

'No I just got here.'

Suddenly thought I had better tell her I'm paying.. Did I pick Judges to show off do you think? Probably. Oh dear, I am no different from her am I?

'My treat' I said, and noticed a brief flicker of relief pass over her face. Mario, the head waiter, gushed effusively as he minced across to greet us.

.'Dear Ms Sutherland, how delightful to see you again so soon, and this **must** be your sister .You are so alike and how beautiful you both are. I will show you to your table, the best one in the restaurant of course.'

Well that was two lies. He tells all his customers their table is the best one in the restaurant, but Helen doesn't know that, and I'm not going to tell her. And the second one is Helen's beautiful but I am definitely not, but we do look alike nevertheless. His remark had pleased Helen no end and she sashayed across the floor to our table as if she owned the place.

Helen

'I'm sure she brought me here to humiliate me. Bitch! It should be me in her position but it's her, the runt of the litter who's Queen Bee these days. We sat down and perused the enormous menu Mario handed us.

'Did you know I worked as a model for a while?' I said, hoping that would impress her.

'No Helen I didn't. Since Mum stopped giving me weekly reports, I have absolutely no idea what you have been up to.' she replied quite sharply.

'Well I did. I was working for a fashion magazine called the *GO GETTER* at the time and I wrote most of the articles too' I continued.

'Did you see me in the documentary on the plight of the whales last night?' Maggie countered. Oh God. I hope we are not going to spend the whole lunch time scoring points off each other. I'm going to stop this right now.

'Do you realise we are doing what we always do, trying to get one over each other. Let's give it a rest and just catch up with what we have been doing over the years, good and bad eh?' Maggie looked a bit sheepish.

'Sorry, yes you're right, let's do that. For starters the last three to four years have been horrendous for me, and I can't imagine yours life hasn't been any better with Richard in prison.' Maggie told me. I gasped; how do you know that? 'Mum told me last time I phoned her.'

'That time with the *GO GETTER* was the best time I ever had in my life,' I told her, but the owner, Ruth's father withdrew his financial support and it had to close. It's Ruth's house where the kids and I are living now. I am teaching at some crap school in a crap part of London, with crap kids who don't want to learn, but I hope it's not for much longer.' I told her, hoping she would come up with a job offer now she knew I could write commercially.

'It's not the kids who are crap it's the parents, who through no fault of their own had a lousy impoverished upbringing themselves, then lived through a war and afterwards had no role models to guide them through the dramatic changes taking place around them. They hoped their children could have a better future than they ever had through education, but what chance have the kids got when they encounter lousy teachers like you, who write them off rather than encouraging them.'

I was furious; who did she think she was, judging me.

.' Lousy teachers, how do you know what kind of a teacher I am?'

'I imagine you're' a Tory -- you sound like one, writing working class kids off like that.'

'You always were a Labourite weren't you?' I challenged her, and leapt to my feet ready to storm out, then hesitated. I wasn't going to be eating a meal of this quality in the foreseeable future, so I bit my tongue, changed the subject, and sat down again to await my starter of goat's cheese and figs on a bed of mixed leaves, not a combination I had encountered before. It was delicious.

Maggie

Helen told me about Richards's problems at the bank and his subsequent arrest. That must have been so humiliating for her. Nobody wants to have to move back in with their parents when they are adult either, and I did genuinely feel sorry for her. It made me realise that in spite of my unhappiness at least I haven't had to worry about money or homelessness to add to my woes. Helen seemed very jealous that I had been living in a manor house in the country; Mum had told her how beautiful it was. I told her.

'Yes, it was beautiful but how would you like to live in a house that looked like a museum set? All it needed was a label stuck on the door stating *Drawing Room circa 1773:* there was not a single piece of furniture, colour scheme or soft furnishing that I had chosen in the entire fifteen or however many rooms there were in the place. You may have been able to make some superficial friends with the pony club brigade, but not me. They were not my type at all, and nor was I their's, so I was desperately lonely. Also I lost my job writing

Maggie's London, because how on earth could I know what was going on in a city that was miles away, in the country with an autistic son – me, a city girl, who had no idea of how to seek help for Michael, or had any one to turn to for help stuck out in the wilds as I was?'

That was a bit disingenuous of me, because I did have Jennifer, but our relationship was a bit complicated to tell Helen about now. She did look at me vaguely sympathetically, saying she had no idea I was so unhappy.

'Is Michael autistic? I didn't know. I have come across one or two at my school. That must be very hard for you?'

She sounded genuine. Maybe there's hope for us yet. Should I tell her I became an alcoholic? Maybe I'll leave that for another time.

Chapter thirty-eight
Divorce 1977 - 1978
Maggie and Helen

Maggie

Divorce is never pleasant, even when both parties are in agreement over the financial arrangements and the visiting rights for their children, -- not that Gerry was too bothered about seeing Michael. He had been to see me in my new home and pleaded with me to try again, but sadly I knew that could never happen. Too much damage had been inflicted on our relationship by my alcoholism and depression, and his neglect and inability to understand my position, and, on reflection, my regrets that I had not been more understanding of his idea of family life as opposed to mine. It's too late now and there was no going back as it would only end in tears again. We cuddled, cried, and hugged each other, we even made love. The parting was so emotional it was inevitable that would happen, but it was a mistake because it almost weakened my resolve.

A deep sadness and sense of loss overwhelmed me when the decree nisi plopped on to the doormat. That was it, -- the finale of what started as a beautiful love affair that we thought would last until the end of our days. I wondered if I would ever fill the void that once contained Gerry. Right now I can't imagine that ever happening. However, I had a job a beautiful house and no money worries, which was a thousand times better than the majority of discarded wives – including Helen. I had a trouble free start for my new life, so I must be positive and get on with it. Come on girl, pull yourself together, onwards and upwards, I told myself, but I didn't feel very upbeat at that moment.

Helen

I wish Richard hadn't looked so pleased when our divorce was granted. When maintenance was discussed, the court sided with Richard and decided because he was an ex-convict, through no fault of his own he had been unable to find work. Therefore he would be unable to make any payments towards the upkeep of his children until he was earning again. After all, his erstwhile wife was a teacher and able to support them herself. Did they have any idea how low teacher's pay was? They didn't seem to realise, or care, there was no way I could afford to keep two children and myself on my salary.' *Through no fault of his own?* Bloody cheek. It wasn't as if I had committed a crime ... **he had**, yet I was the one being punished. Ruth, bless her heart, was incredibly generous, and even told me to stop the money I was now paying into her bank account every month. Mind you, she did put her foot down when she realised I was still buying my kids clothes in Harrods – well I always had, so it hadn't really occurred to me to look elsewhere for them.

'You're behaving as if you are still the wife of a Financial Director' she told me.

'You should look round some of the charity shops; you would be amazed what you can find there, particularly in a well off area like this.' Charity shops? I was horrified. 'How dare you suggest such a thing' I chided her, and stomped off out of the room? She was chuckling to herself as I left. I don't know what was so funny about it. I'm going to have to find myself a new husband. — Not any old husband, a financially sound one. Never mind all that romantic rubbish. I can live without that. Security is top of the list now. I think it's the only way I am going to get out the rut that I'm in. But, where am I going to find this Lothario? Certainly not at that crappy school I work in, something has to change.

Chapter thirty-nine
Maggie 1978

Sometime later Gerry came to see me at the Fulham house and he seemed ill at ease.

'I need to tell you something he said because I don't want you to find out about it from tabloids.'

'Find out about what? Come on in Gerry, spit it out.'

'I'm getting married again'. .

I was taken aback. Stupid really as I had seen pictures of him in the papers with a tall willowy snooty looking debutante type, and as he was now free and was quite a catch, it was inevitable some woman was going to grab him fairly soon.

'Oh, is that the girl I have seen with you in the papers?'

'Yes, her name is the Jane Russtington Bridges. Her father is a Viscount.' he said rather sheepishly.

'So she's an Honourable. Not another common bird like me' I laughed. 'Good luck Gerry. I really do wish you all the best and sincerely hope you will be happy'.

'Thank you, you're very sweet, and there's something else I need to tell you and you are not going to like it. I'm going to stand for Parliament.'

'Brilliant. You always said you would do that when the time was right.' Why does he think I'm not going to like it?

'Oh my God, you've turned blue.' I challenged him, 'Yes you have. I can see it in your face. Has your new wife to be turned you into Tory boy? I did wonder sometimes if your political stance when we were together was just to please me, because you knew how committed I was?'

'No I promise you, I was genuinely far more on the left then, but times have changed, and what was best for the country then is not what is the best thing now.'

I was about to embark on a sea of political rhetoric but decided against it. What did it matter what his views were. It was nothing to do with me anymore.

'I expect they will give you a safe seat because of who you are.' I hope he picks up the sarcasm in my voice. 'Canvassing can be pretty tough you know.' I told him. 'You get called some nasty names, particularly if you're wearing a blue rosette. The Labour voters are not as polite as your lot if you knock on their doors.' I thought I would put him on the spot.

'Are you going to say hello to Michael while you're here? He has made considerable progress since he started at the new school. He'll never be cured because it's not that kind of condition, but he is much easier to live with now, providing we stick to a routine.'

'Sorry, in a bit o a rush today, bye, I still love you lots you know.' he said and rushed out of the front door. Bastard! He's getting married yet he wants to make sure I continue to hanker after him and so I don't get involved with anyone else. I think he has turned into one of those men who are always in love with the one before. I am beginning to realise just how shallow Gerry is. Not his fault really. It's because he is golden boy. Good looking, posh, rich, talented and adored He had never had to deal with a crisis in his life until I blew a gasket and Michael wasn't quite what he expected his heir would be like. I needed to sound off to somebody so I phoned Alex who had become a close friend. He was laughing at me

'Slow down your gabbling. Fancy a trip to Richmond for lunch?' he asked.

He took me by surprise, but I called up to Pat to see if she wouldn't mind keeping an eye on Michael for a couple of hours so I was able to join him. It was a beautiful day and Richmond was looking its best. We went to a pub by the river and sat outside watching the swans and the pleasure boats sail by, it was idyllic and all my anger floated away on the movement of the water. Alex was such an easy guy to be with.

'I do love being with you', I told him. 'Everything seems so simple after the traumatic world I inhabited before I came back to London.'

'Maggie you could be with me forever if you wanted to. You must know how I feel about you; everybody else in the office has guessed.' He took my breath away: what do I respond to that?

'No, I didn't realise: I don't know what to say. I have only ever seen you as a dear friend. and my boss. I'm really sorry I blurted out. He looked cress fallen and the carefree atmosphere of the day evaporated. We were both slightly embarrassed and I spluttered that I had better get back now to relieve Pat telling him Michael was hard going after having him for too long.

'Sorry, I've messed thing up haven't I?'

'No Alex you haven't, but I really must get home.' I mumbled. In the evening lounging on my sofa, I thought this is where orange juice doesn't quite hit the spot as I could do with a very large glass of Merlot right now. I needed to talk to someone about this turn of events; so I gave Sheila a ring. Since my return to London Sheila and I had teamed up again just like we had in the past, and were best mates all over again. She was married an old school friend of ours, David, and had two kids, and naturally we had been bridesmaids at each other's weddings. That was back in my happy days in Notting Hill. I was God mother to Sally and Sam, and she was to Michael along with countless other snooty 'bods chosen by Gerry and his mother, which seemed to be the thing in aristocratic families Maybe it was a way of making a claim for a mention in the will when they popped off.

'Hi love, I've' got myself into a tricky situation.

'Oh yeah, so what's'' new Sheila said.

'Alex, my boss, has just declared his love for me'.

Sheila roared with laughter. You sound like some Victorian maiden for God's sake.

He's lovely – marry him.'

'We haven't even kissed yet.'

'Well get on with it then. When was the last time you had sex? You were never so reticent in the past to bed your blokes. Give him a ring now she ordered,' so I did.

'Alex I'm so sorry the way I reacted to you today. You took me by surprise, and I didn't know how to react. Please come over to my place so I can apologise properly.'

He didn't wait to be asked and broke all records getting here.

Chapter forty
Helen 1979

I had been a paid up member of the Conservative Party for some time now, and I was over the moon when the chairman of the local group asked me if I would consider standing as a candidate in the forthcoming local council elections in May. I didn't hesitate and agreed straight away. I liked the idea of being called Councillor Mrs Sutherland- Capstic.

'Thank you so much for asking me Cllr Jones,' I gushed 'You know how devoted I am to the party' Oh dear, I think I might have over done that a bit. I fancied myself attending functions as an important member of the local community, but being a novice at this sort of thing, I forgot that first I have to be elected, which involves a massive amount of work such as traipsing round the streets delivering leaflet after leaflet, and knocking on countless doors, only to have some of them slammed in my face. How rude the proletariat are.

Cllr Jones told me 'It's what we call a derelict ward, and needs a lot of work to build up support.' Omitting to tell me the chances of winning there were zero. I had to go for an interview with the volunteers in my ward, all two of them -- to confirm my selection. I was beginning to wish I hadn't been quite so keen to stand but didn't know how to wriggle out of it. 'I do have a slight problem' I told to my interrogators, 'I have two children and a full time job, so consequently I am a bit limited time wise.' Cllr Jones must have heard me. 'Call me Rupert' he said No need for formalities here; don't worry the rest of us will help you.' Hindsight is a wonderful thing isn't it? If I had made a bit of an effort to work on previous elections, I might have had more of an idea of just what is entailed when you are a candidate in a derelict ward, and .that you don't get **any** help.

I am afraid I flirted with Rupert outrageously during the campaign so he actually delivered most of my leaflets for me, silly old fool. Then I had an outrageous piece of luck. An ancient member who had represented a strongly Tory ward for what seemed like the beginning of time, died. He was in his nineties and looked ten years older. He had become a liability to the party as he had a habit of falling asleep in meetings, and had to be prodded to wake him up to vote. Well, at last Fridays planning meeting Cllr Russell had to prod him a bit harder than usual and he fell off his chair and on to the floor -- dead. He had probably been that way for some time, but as he tended to look as if he had expired anyway, nobody noticed that he actually had. I was invited to step into the void he had left and stand as the conservative candidate in his ward. I won the seat with very little effort on my part, as it was the bluest ward in the constituency. I thought it would look a bit sad if I took my Mum to the count, and even sadder if I went on my own so I asked David, one of the teachers at my school to come with me, which he was delighted to do.

Well, so much for the jollies I thought I would be attending? My life is now one of continual round of meetings, with people getting all het up over endless trivia. Not much fun actually, and Rupert is constantly up close and personal. Ugh! And then there are the constituents. They all want to park outside their own house, for nothing of course, and for me to evict a neighbour that they don't feel is quite good enough for their area. Selfish lot! Where's their sense of community?

Chapter forty-one
Maggie 1980/81

Alex and I desperately want to set up home together but I am concerned about Michael's reaction to somebody else moving into the house, as he can be very hostile to strangers. We will have to stay in my home rather than Alex's so as not to upset his routine, which even though he is so much easier to live with now, he can still explode and smash the place up by throwing anything he can get his hands on at the walls. Pat tells me it happens when he feels insecure or is experiencing sensory overload. He's fifteen now and towers above me, being tall like his father. He's used to me not being around all the time, but if Pat stays out overnight with her new boyfriend Jake, Michael freaks out by wandering all over the house calling for her. However the wonderful school he now attends tell me he could possibly be trained to do a simple routine type of job as he has progressed so much recently.

Something like checking stock in and out of a small warehouse. I would love it if he could.

His life is so narrow and restricted. Home school, home school: it's not stimulating enough for a growing lad.

I plucked up courage and introduced Alex to him, which was not a huge success. Michael has a way of standing back and giving an unfriendly sideways glance at new people, often followed by 'I don't like you,' in a snarling voice, then he retreats upstairs to his room.. Because I love Alex, I had hoped Michael would take to him instantly, but of course he didn't, and he gave Alex the usual hostile treatment.

'Are you sure you want to live with me?' I asked him after Michael's rejection.

'You bet I do. Well get there in the end he said optimistically.' I hope he's right because I'm absolutely crazy about the man, and can't wait to share my life with him completely. I'm so happy now with my life – it frightens me some times as I'm terrified it will all fall apart again. I love Alex, my job, my house, living in London again, it's all too wonderful, and I am terrified of sinking back into a pit of despair again.

Three months later

We are finally living together in my house. Michael ignored him for the first few weeks and stormed upstairs running a ruler up the banisters making a hell of a racket whenever he came into the house. Then slowly, slowly, he gradually got used to him being there, and actually started to talk to him in his strange way. Last night he asked him if he was his father. I jumped in quickly and told him 'No darling, Gerry is your father: do you remember him?' He rolled his eyes, took his time and said **No** loudly. He paused before he spoke as always, then he told me all his friends at school have fathers, and they take them out for picnics.

'Why doesn't my father take me out for picnics? He asked. Whatever could I say to the poor love? Not the truth that's for sure which is he doesn't love you or even like you, and is embarrassed by you. Darling Alex chipped in before I could come up with an answer, and asked him 'Would you like your mum and me to take you on a picnic?'

I should have told Alex that you never get a direct answer from Michael. He needs time to mull over what you have asked him, rolling his eyes whilst he thinks it through. 'Ooo yes' he eventually answered' with a big smile on his face. I did wonder if he knew what a picnic was but he obviously did as he offered to help me make sandwiches. I hesitated at first as in his strange way of reasoning, he thinks brown bread is dirty, so whenever he sees it he throws it on the floor and stamps on it, .and if I am not quick enough, he will grab the whole loaf and throw it in the bin. Alex and I both prefer wholemeal bread. Oh well, I'd better make them all white to save further agro. Life isn't straight forward living with my son.

It was September 1981 and the Women's Peace Movement was gathering followers in their hundreds to protest at the placement of American nuclear Cruise missiles on an RAF base at Greenham Common. I told our team this was going to be a BIG story, and I had no intention of missing out on it.

'I'm going up there to interview some of the women'. I told them. There's a human story there with women leaving their families because they feel so strongly against the proliferation of these weapons.'

'Surely you are not going to stay there overnight in all that mud?' someone said. Not sure who.

'Careful Mag's, they're all dykes up there' Sid Green said, laughing at his witticism. I had a strong urge to hit him, I had never had him down as a bigot, but I gritted my teeth as I needed to keep him on my side as he was our senior cameraman, and I may have to work with him on this story – IF I could persuade the guys it was worth following up.

'Of course I'm going to stay. How else will I find out how they live in such hostile conditions, and how the police, the Yanks and the council are treating them unless I do?' I told them.

'Go for it girl' Andy, our director piped up 'It sounds like a great idea to me.' Alex looked worried, but didn't attempt to stop me going. If he had I would have reminded him the sort of investigative journalist I used to be, and why he wanted to employ me in the first place

I bought an ancient van so I would look like another supporter rather than a nosey journalist and I did wonder at one point if it would get me to Greenham it made so many splutters and groans along the way. It ground to a halt when I arrived and I wondered if it would ever leap into life again.

'Hi I'm Maggie'. I called out to a nearby girl.

'First visit? Park over there luv. I'm Jill. Welcome to Greenham.' The van sprang back into life much to my surprise and Jill jumped in beside me to direct me to a space and then took me to meet some of the girls. I use the word girls, but there were all ages there, even some octogenarians roughing it. Amazing.

'This is Becca; she is the nearest thing we have to a leader on this particular site'. Jill told me. 'We don't have leaders here, I'm just the one with the loudest mouth,' she added. I decided to come clean and tell Becca my reason for being here.

'I want to get to know some of you as individuals, not the way the press portray you as a mass of screaming lesbians.' She gave me a very hostile look.

'.I want to know your backgrounds and why you feel so strongly against these weapons that so many of you have left your families and your comfortable homes to come here to protest against the threat they pose to mankind.' That was a bit over the top I thought. I hope I sounded sincere.

'We've had too many journalists round here, being all nice and then slagging us off in their shit newspapers thank you. Why don't you piss off home.' Becca chastised me. Oh dear, not a good start I thought: wrong tactics.

'Aren't you Maggie Sutherland?' One of Becca's sidekicks piped up.' I used to read your column years ago.'

'Yes I am and if you read my articles you will know I'm not in the business of condemning people for fighting for their beliefs.' Becca defrosted, ever so slightly.

'The company I work for would like to make a film of your attempts to alert the world to the dangers in developing these wicked weapons.' I informed her.

Suddenly they were all talking to me at once and asking me what sort of film I wanted to make. Amazing how many people want to see themselves on TV. Becca relented. Phew!

'You will have to let us see your film before we allow it to be shown on TV, and if any of the girls change their minds about appearing in it your report, you will have to respect their wishes, or we will sue you.' That told me where to get off..

I think she was trying to intimidate me and drew herself up to her full height as she announced this. She wasn't that tall, but it's not difficult to tower over me.

I told her 'You will have full editing rights I promise you, and the film company will draw up a legal contract agreeing to all your concerns.'

'We've got a solicitor,' she said 'Gillian Russell. She works for us for nothing as her contribution to the cause.'

Alex and I met Gillian in her in her chambers in Lincolns Inn, and signed all the papers she had prepared to save her clients from wicked journalists. I'm really excited to start the project, and will set off again tomorrow. This time I took a hand held camera and spoke to as many of the women as I could. I found out Greenham was made up of a series of camps around the airbase Some of the protesters lived on the site permanently, sleeping under leaky tents and tarpaulin: some slept rough wrapped only in plastic; others came in caravans whenever they could manage for a few days, and at the weekends women turned up in their hundreds to support the cause. I felt a huge surge of excitement and empathy for these women living in such awful conditions for their deeply held beliefs.

They were fighting for a nuclear free world: a campaign I was happy to be associated with.

'Next time I come I told Becca, I will bring masses of supplies for you. Give me a list of things that you are most in need of.'

I met Elizabeth, who was an academic, and was defying her professor by coming here. Mild mannered Gladys was a fruit and veg stall holder from Borough Market. She left her husband to manage the stall and the kids in order to join the protesters, and he was quite happy to support his wife so she could do her bit.

'I'm just so angry that our government have put us all at risk by allowing the bloody Americans to bring these horrific weapons into the UK.' A young girl in the crowd said.

'They're supposed to be a deterrent, that's a joke,' somebody at the back of the crowd that had gathered around me shouted. I felt invigorated by the enthusiasm and dedication to the cause, and couldn't wait to begin filming.

Jill introduced me to Gloria.' Martin, my husband, is a lazy sod: he hasn't done a stroke of work for years' – she said, 'it'll do him good to take some responsibility for the home instead of me doing everything.' Jill told me Martin had threatened her by saying he would leave if she went to Greenham with all those lefties and lesbians, hoping to frighten her into submission, but Gloria was having none of it and gathered up her four kids and brought them to the camp with her.. There was a safe area away from the traffic at the back of the airfield where the mothers and children camped. The stories kept on coming. Rosie's husband beat her to a pulp the first time she came because she wasn't there to give him his tea when he came home from work. 'Well he can bloody well get it himself from now on, as I am not going back to him'. Rosie told me that many of the husbands were supportive of their wives and a few of them brought supplies to the camp as their way of helping the protesters' she added. One thing I discovered they all had in common was whatever their background or political views, was their total commitment to the cause to rid the world of nuclear weapons.

Back at the office and looking the material Stan our senior photographer and I had filmed I was thrilled.

'Guys look at this' I whooped; 'This is going to be a real winner.'

I persuaded my colleagues to postpone the film until December as something really big was planned.

'Don't be daft, I'll be old hat by then,' piped up Richy, one of the researchers.

'What's going to happen then anyway? I had to confess I didn't know as only the leaders of the protest did, and had hinted as much to me.

'Well that's no bloody good is it? This time it was Stan, who didn't like me. I could understand him in a way. As far as he was concerned, I was the bosses bit of crumpet, throwing her weight around.

'There's loads of activity we can film before that' I said, my voice sounding a bit high. There's a blockade with two hundred and fifty women throwing themselves in front of the lorries planned. That's happening next week. Women chaining themselves to the perimeter fence and. 'You're getting a real bossy boots since you've been going up there'. Stan said partly in jest.

'Sorry, didn't mean to dictate, but I'm really excited by this project.

'That's OK, only joking.' No he wasn't.: I'd better tread carefully here. I don't want them to think I'm taking over. Alex grinned but said nothing. At home later he told me as far as he was concerned Greenham was my project

'But the guys are not ready for a woman boss he said, so be subtle how you deal with them.' 'Me subtle? That'll be a first. Amazing, the UK has a woman Prime Minister, but men still hate taking orders from a women in the work place' I snapped. Lying in bed later I remembered how I had allowed myself to be crushed into submission not that long ago, and it was darling Alex who had brought me back to life. I turned to him, covering him with kisses.

'Park here Stan, What's going on over there?' I shouted at him. A full scale war had broken out Newbury Council bailiffs, assisted by the police, were endeavouring to evict the women, and it was turning into a blood bath.

'Stan, don't stand there gawping, get filming.'

'Gaw'd the cops are being a bit heavy 'anded 'aint they?' he said.

'Yes, it's not the first time I've seen this happen, but this is on a grander scale. 'Look over there' I yelled, That copper is beating up that young girl. Film it.'

Suddenly I found myself pinned face down in the mud being arrested and handcuffed. Another police officer had got Stan in a headlock and another one was pulling the film out of the camera and stamping it in the mud.

'You vicious bastards', I yelled as they dragged me away to spend the night in a police cell. Cameras flashed taking pictures of me, not exactly looking my best.

Alex picked us up the following day after our court appearance where the pair of us were fined for causing a breach of the peace.

'Not a good idea to antagonise the police' Alex chastised me. 'Now every time you show your face they will be on to you. We're not going to be able to get a lot of new footage then.'

'Sorry, I said sheepishly, but I wasn't. I am determined to tell the true story of Greenham and I will find a way around this little hiccup.

Chapter forty-two
Helen 1981

I see the bitch is hitting the headlines again. She's on the front page of the INFORMER and other Nationals, being dragged off to prison looking an absolute fright.' I was at Mum's, who was upset by Maggie's latest exploits. The photograph was a deliberately unflattering one, presenting her as a rabid unwashed communist agitator.

'It's that awful job she has' Mum said sadly. 'Why can't she have a respectable one like you darling?' Respectable is that how she sees being a teacher? It might have been once upon a time, but with all these children's rights being fashionable, it certainly isn't now. We have become the enemy. Mum would never comprehend exactly just what Maggie had achieved. Just as well from my point of view, as I am her favourite, and maybe wouldn't be if she realised. She only understands the old conventional lists of jobs like the Civil Service, Doctors, and Teachers and of course people who had degrees; they are the jobs that represented success to her, not the world Maggie lives in. If only she knew how I envied her.

'Why have the police changed from being kind to beating people up?' Mum questioned. 'Why can't the miners get on with their job instead of refusing to work, and surely those cruise missile things are only here to protect us? Thank goodness we have Charles and Diana's wedding to look forward to in July.' Then out of the blue she announced,

'Maggie is on television tonight. Did you know?'

'What programme?' I snapped

'That political one on BBC two.' What does her opinion matter to anyone, particularly after this latest debacle? That's it I'm off home. 'Sorry mum -- got to dash.'

I thought it was time to consider my future again, rather like Richard and I had all those years ago. OK, maybe that didn't turn out quite the way I'd hoped, with the idiot man getting himself banged up, but the idea was solid. If you don't like the way things are, change them. Mum, of all people, had said that to me years ago. Back at school the next day I thought the time was right to ensnare David, the new English teacher. I have come to the conclusion I will be better off with a husband and he would fit the bill nicely. Well educated, presentable, nice manners: yes just the ticket.

'Morning David, did you have a good weekend?' I asked tilting my head slightly, and focusing my big blue eyes firmly on him. At lunch time he asked did I fancy a drink after work. You bet I did, but mustn't seem too keen.

'Sorry, can't make tonight' I lied, but I'm free tomorrow.'

Never mind *after school*, not romantic enough, so I switched the meeting to the evening. He seemed enthusiastic. Am I getting there? Hope so.

Good old Ruth looked after the children for me. I made sure the evening was a success, so it was followed up with regular meetings; the poor guy getting more involved after each date – or so I thought.

'What do your parents do?' I asked coyly one evening, moving my plan up a level. No point in pursing him if he was penniless.

'Oh Dad's an accountant and Mum looks after the family.'

'Does he work for one of the big city companies?'

'Oh no. He has his own practice. He always wanted me to join him but he would always treat me as a kid, so no way.'

'Perhaps he needs your support?' I ventured.

'Too bad, he's already got about twenty Chartered Accountants working for him so he doesn't need me.' Wow, money in the family so I turned the charm up several notches.

The weeks went by and I felt I wasn't getting anywhere. He should have weakened by now. Why was he not trying to get me into bed? Was he gay?

'Shall we go to the theatre this week-end?' I suggested brightly.

'No I can't I'm afraid. I'm going to Paris to see my family.'

That was a surprise. 'Do your parents live there?'

'No my wife and children do' I couldn't believe what I was hearing.

'You're married you bastard leading me on like that' I spluttered.

'I told you I had two children: I thought you would realise my wife would be looking after them whilst I studied for my Diploma. In fact I remember you saying, I bet your wife is babysitting when I asked you out for a drink the first time.' Shit, that's true I had forgotten that.

'What Diploma? I thought you were an English teacher here'. I challenged him. 'Only for a term: I needed to work in a deprived inner city school as part of my course. I'm really sorry if you thought we had a future together. I love my wife and family dearly, and as for me leading you on, I think it might be the other way round, don't you?'

I stormed off back to Ruth's. 'The bastard's married.' I yelled as if it was her fault. 'Which bastard is this darling?' She asked sarcastically.

'David of course.'

'All men are bastards, I told you that before.' Ruth exclaimed. 'Women are best. I told you that too -- when you first slept with me -- and you agreed then. What made you think men have changed in that short time? I flounced off to my own room feeling humiliated – again.

Chapter forty-three
Maggie 1982

'Maggie McIntyre, I don't want to live with you anymore.' Alex announced grinning from ear to ear. I panicked, why? What did he mean? I thought we were getting on well. Why is he grinning? 'I want to live with you as my wife.' He announced. I sighed with relief.

'What brought that on?' I asked.

'Shall we say -- love?'

I thought about it – briefly I have to say. 'If you really want me to marry you, then yes you big lump, of course I will, because I love you too.'

'Fantastic. Well get a special licence.' he enthused. I thought about my poor mum, who had had a raw deal with both her daughters as far as weddings were concerned. Maybe I should give her the wedding she always envisaged, for one of us at least.

'Darling, I owe her big time after my marriage to Gerry.' I told Alex. 'It was not one of the best moments of my life and I feel ashamed to tell you what I did. I lied to Gerry by saying my parents lived in Spain, and were not in very good health at the time and couldn't come. Mum and Dad found out about our marriage in the COURIER: we were on the front page because Gerry was a bit of a celebrity.'

I could feel myself blushing with shame as I told him. He looked a bit surprised by my behaviour: I think he still has me on a pedestal. Oh dear, I'm not really pedestal material; I hope he is not going to be too disappointed when he knows me better. Then he smiled.

'Well get a special licence I can't wait to marry you in case you change your mind, and we will definitely ask your parents, and mine as well and anyone else you're mum might want to ask.' Maybe this is my chance to make amends and involve her in some of the organisation. Would you mind love? I warn you it will be awful.'

'Course not, anything you want. As a matter of interest why didn't you ask her to your nuptials? She is your Mum, and you know how mums get excited about their kids getting married.'

'Because I was being a snobby selfish bitch and have felt ashamed about it ever since.

I set the date for June 10th, Helen's and my forty fourth birthday. Mum was overjoyed when I asked her to organise the reception.

'Don't' go over the top I begged her. After all we have both been married before.

'I will ask all the relatives you should have asked to your first shindig, but were too frightened that we weren't posh enough for your new show biz so called friends.' She replied bitterly. Oh dear, I thought she may have got over the snub by now, but obviously not.

'OK mum: ask whoever you like.' Mum took me at my word and threw herself into the preparations making list after list of aunts, uncles, cousins and any number of people I had never heard of to the do. She wanted to have the reception in that bloody hotel in the High Street that she thinks is so wonderful and I hate, but I bit my tongue and said nothing. Alex thought the whole thing was hugely comical and didn't interfere. My dad said he thought she had mistaken her remit, and thought she was organizing Charles and Diana's forth coming bonanza, the amount of time she was devoting to our wedding.

She phoned me up in tears one day to tell me Helen had declined her invitation with the feeble excuse that it was imperative she should fulfil a long time arrangement to speak at a conference in the day, and that some friends had booked a meal in a smart restaurant to celebrate her birthday in the evening, so she couldn't come.

'I told her family is always more important than friends but she wouldn't listen.' Did she have any friends? I wondered. Mum said the only one she had ever mentioned was Ruth. She's probably jealous. Speaking at a conference? Who is she trying to kid.

I popped round to see how Mum was getting on with the arrangements and overheard Dad and Mum talking.

'I suppose I will be expected to pay for this pantomime, so you can cut that list in half right now René.' I heard him say. He only ever called her Rene when he was cross with her. It was always darling, sweetheart, or mother. Poor old Dad: I really should have told him Alex and I always intended to pay. I was making my getaway but I could still hear him going on at Mum.

'As for this table plan you are making such a drama about, I would say seeing as you don't know most of these so called relatives on that list, and have no idea which one's are not speaking to each for some reason or other, you may well put arch enemies on the same table. That'll be fun, and as for your favourite daughter not coming, you should have insisted that she did. ' Favourite eh? Dad had noticed. I was never sure whether he had or not. I sidled off quietly for five minutes and then re-entered making a lot of noise clattering through the back door.

'Hi everyone, I called out I've come round to give you some money for anything you have had to pay out for.' I shouted. Poor old dad, I should have realised that as 'Father of the Bride' he would think he would have to finance this wedding. I gave him a few signed cheques making it clear Alex and I were paying. Bless Dad, he looked very relieved. I think I am going to take over the table plan – subtly of course. Can't have our mates and colleagues sitting out in the corridor and all these unknown relatives right up front can we?'

I woke up on my wedding day after a sleepless night and with a feeling of dread. I am marrying a man I adore, and want to spend the rest of my life with, so why am I feeling this way? I think it's because I don't think I am much good at being a wife, and I would hate to disappoint Alex. He deserves better and I wish he hadn't wanted to change our relationship.

We were very happy as we were so why spoil things? I was thinking about my marriage to Gerry. Although I would like to blame him for what went wrong, it wasn't entirely his fault our partnership broke down. In retrospect, I think I could have made a bit more of an effort to settle into the Big House. How many brides get a chance to move into a magnificent Regency mansion, furnished with priceless antiques? Not many I bet, but all I did was moan about it.

Shall I call the whole thing off? Whatever would Mum say if I did? All those unknown bods she has invited, the shame of it. Who's that banging on the door? It was Sheila, my maid of honour. That's a daft silly name for this day and age.

'You're going to be late. What are you doing still in bed? Get up you lazy cow, we've got to get you looking fantastic, and that's going to take a while. You're looking decidedly ropey at the moment.' She said. I looked at the clock and couldn't believe the time. I had overslept on the most important day of my life.

'Sorry, last minute nerves I suppose. Right let's turn this ugly duckling into a swan. Mum's going to have a fit when she sees this dress. She wants me in some pastel horror. I had chosen an amazing creation by Zandra Rhodes as my wedding dress. It was a mixture of scarlet purple and other brilliant colours in geometric juxtapositions and had practically bankrupted me. But, wow, what a dress!'

The Registry Office was so full that many of the guests couldn't find a spare chair to sit on, and were standing at the back of the -- not very big room, looking sulky. 'Gawd. Who are all these people? Mum had invited the entire northern section of the Sutherland clan along with her relatives the Rushton's, plus all of Alex's staff and anyone who had ever worked for him on an ad hoc basis (Where did she get their addresses from?) and even some of Gerry's BBC mates: highly embarrassing. I was surprised to see she hadn't included the staff from the supermarket too. What was I thinking off handing the whole wedding over to Mum?' Unknown guests kept pouncing on me at the reception gushing over me. I recognised Uncle

Charlie. 'Eee lass, that's some dress. It's more suitable for a carnival than a wedding isn't it?' Then roared with laughter at his silly joke.

'Saw you on TV darling, talking to those awful Greenham women.' a tiny person with a northern accent said. I opened my mouth to squash this unknown creature and then decided against it knowing I could never win against deep rooted prejudice like hers, and left her standing.

'Large lady approaching stage left,' Alex whispered, grinning for ear to ear. He was finding the whole thing hysterically comic. I wish I could see the funny side of it.

'Darling, lovely to see you again: you're the clever one aren't you?' this unknown person gushed.

'Sorry to disappoint you I replied. I'm the other one.'

'Oh I remember now, you were a bit of a let-down to your mother weren't you'? Gritting my teeth I told her this is MY wedding you're attending, and I don't remember ever meeting you, so I have no idea why my Mother invited you. I wouldn't have done so I can assure you' I informed her as I flounced off. Alex beat a hasty retreat and went across to his parents so he could laugh out loud, pretending his father had made a joke. I joined them seething.

'There's that bloody degree rearing its head again,' I told Alex's Mum, Sally.'

'She judges everything I've ever done against that, and I'm always found wanting. I swear the first thing she ever says to any one she meets is *my daughter Helen's got a first class degree.* It's sickening.'

'I wouldn't let it worry you darling. We think you're clever and pretty special. There are not many girls who could wear that dress with such panache, and that includes your sister?' she told me. Naturally mum hated it, and thought I was wearing it just to embarrass her. Perhaps I was?

I loved Alex's family. His father was a lecturer at a Teacher Training College: his mother was head Mistress of a Secondary School, and his brother James was a Head Master somewhere or other. Alex had also started his career as a teacher until he moved on to the BBC eventually leaving to start his own film company.

'Unimaginative lot aren't we?' his Dad pronounced. It's as if we couldn't think of anything else to do other than be teachers.' Mum came across to speak to them.

'I hope you are enjoying yourselves' she asked, defying them to say otherwise. I asked, her who are all these people you have asked especially that rude northern woman over there?'

'Oh she's your Uncle Jack's sister in law's ex husband's new wife.' The McDonald clan exploded with laughter. Mum looked bemused.

'Why did they think that was funny? I don't like them, they're rude.'

'I **love** them' I countered. As soon as Alex and I were able we fled the reception. We went to Brighton for a couple of days, then on to New York for two or three weeks. The films Alex had produced so far had been very parochial and he was keen to develop a market outside the UK, so we used the honeymoon to combine business and pleasure, but with an emphasis on pleasure.

Chapter forty-four
Maggie 1982 / 83

The women had declared the camp to be 'Women Only' in February. I wasn't too happy about that on two counts. They had received a tremendous support and physical help from lots of men, also I thought it gave ammunition to the press to support their view that the camp was run by a lot of left wing lesbians. Rubbish of course, but difficult to refute after banning men. I visited the camp throughout the summer and involved myself in the huge task of sending out chain letters to thousands of women inviting them to take part in creating a circle around the airbase to protest against the proliferation of nuclear weapons. This was the big one I had asked the boys to delay our report for.

The response was a staggering **thirty thousand women** joined hands to completely encircle the nine mile perimeter fence.

'That'll knock 'em dead' an excited Becca shouted to me

'Make a note of the date you lot' Jill yelled to the press 'December 12th 1982. It's a day history will remember when women **made you** listen to them about the danger these evil weapons will cause to world peace.'

Jill was a tiny little women from the north of England, but what she lacked in height, she made up for in courage, determination and dedication to the cause. She had been present at every major protest; she'd had a policeman's baton smashed across her back, bruising her badly, and had lost everything she possessed when Newbury council had trashed the camp. She wouldn't let me film her, but she did contribute to the sound track of our film. None of us knew anything about her home life, which may have had something to do with her refusal to be filmed. Alex and the team were there in force at the protest, and the Greenham women's peace campaign was finally taken seriously, gaining a massive increase in support throughout the world. The production team rushed back to London and worked through the night completed our documentary, and Alex managed to create a bidding war between the major TV companies to buy the rights to show it. The BBC won, and was shown the following week to much acclaim.

February 1983

Wow, our film on the Peace Camp won the best documentary award at the BAFTA's the following February. We were elated. I drove up to the camp to tell the women about THEIR success and to invite everyone involved to a massive THANK YOU party at a top London hotel to celebrate. I managed to get contact addresses of the ones who were no longer at the camp for one reason or another, as I didn't want to miss anybody who had helped out, and told them we would arrange transport for them.

'Are you proud of your mum?' Alex asked Becca's kids aged nine and ten at the party.' Her husband Steve had looked after the family when she was at the camp, but Becca answered Alex, as her family seemed to be struck dumb.

'They think that's the end of it now and I will be coming home, and they were not best pleased when I said I won't do that until these killer missiles are removed from the UK soil.'

Becca and I had become good friends over the past year, and I was worried about her family's future in view of their inability to answer Alex's question. I expressed my concern to her when we were alone.

'Yeah, I know she replied, Steve is getting pissed off with the situation, so I think I am going to eat my words and serve in some other way in the future.' She looked sad, and I know she will miss the drama of life in the camp.

'Maybe I can still come up at the week-ends?' she said cheerfully. I remember early in our association, asking her where she worked pre Greenham.

'I worked in a super-market.' she laughed. 'A little mouse in a job for little mice who jumped every time the 'boss cat' appeared'. I couldn't imagine her in such a humdrum job. Was I being a snob? No I don't think so. I just wondered how many of the leaders at Greenham, who had flowered amongst the mud and privation of the camp achieving personal success, -- what had their lives been like before? I decided I would write a book about them – if I can ever find the time.

Chapter forty-five
Helen and Maggie 1985 - 1990

Maggie

Alex and I had bought a cottage on the banks of the river Parret in Somerset.

Yes I know – who was never going to set foot in the countryside ever again, except for work? ME. But he convinced me we needed a retreat for some uninterrupted time to plan our new productions, and just for the two of us to get away occasionally as there were too many distractions in London. Initially I had said he could stay there on his own as there was no way I would set foot in the country to live again even for a short time, but he assured me It would be completely different from my previous experience of country living, because both of us are dedicated Londoners, and we would always have our home in the city.

'I remember those red coated murderers meeting at the pub before they embarked on their killing spree,' I told him. 'Gerry expected me to meet him at the pub with all the other Hooray Henries and Henriettas before they set off to murder some poor creature. **Not bloody likely**, I abhor killing animals for sport. I wouldn't go, nor would I speak to him for two or three days after he had been on a hunt.'

'OK Eliza, well make sure we don't buy anywhere they have an established Hunt. I was imaging something more peaceful like us having lunch in pretty country pubs watching the river flow by.' 'Sorry love,' I interrupted, 'I was just thinking about the horror I felt seeing the terrified fox tearing across the fields with the baying of dogs and hunters relishing the chase. It made my blood boil.' Feeling duly chastised, I gave in. He was right, and I really must learn to engage brain and think things through before I start yelling.

My darling Alex will join me in a couple of hours, and I am so pleased I gave in to him over the cottage. We were always surrounded with people at work and at home, and he was right, it was bliss for just the two of us to get away from the hustle and bustle occasionally. I was lolling in a deckchair in our cottage garden which is miles from anywhere, sunning myself listening to the river lapping at bank and watching the ducks going about their business. Bliss! I would never have thought I, but then I have never felt so content in all my life.

Did I ever really love Gerry I asked myself, and why was my love for Alex so different? Of course I loved him, who wouldn't? He was Prince Charming? Rich, aristocratic, successful, handsome, every girls dream, and he was in love with me. I suppose I was proud of myself for reeling in such a catch, but we should never have married. That was when reality set in and our differences reared their ugly heads. It's different with Alex. We are totally relaxed and honest with each other and have the same beliefs on what is important in our lives. I'm so lucky.

Helen

I lost my seat at the local elections. The electorate are a miserable lot. It doesn't matter what you do for them it's never enough. I truly hate them. To rub it in Maggie's triumphs always seem to coincide with my failures. Even Mum's bragging about her achievement to the neighbours: that's got to be a first.

'Did you see my daughter on television etc . . . Dad told me not to take my loss too hard.

'You can put a rosette on a donkey, and if it is the right political colour for the time, the donkey will win.' he said. The sickening thing is the Tories are on a roll because of Margaret Thatcher's gung ho reaction to Argentina's threat against the UK over who owned the Falkland Islands, which appears to have aroused patriotism in so many people, so I shouldn't have lost. BUT the bloody County Council, against the advice of the Borough where I was a councillor, had committed an unforgivable sin by giving planning permission for a hundred and forty houses to be built on the only open space in my ward where the kids could play, so against the national trend, we –or rather **I,** was punished., and we lost control of the council. Maggie has just phoned me attempting to sound sorry and commiserate with me. Bitch.'

She's delighted I'm sure hoping this Labour win could be the beginning of further gains in the Country. It wasn't Ha ha. Then she surprised me.

'I'm going down to the cottage this week-end as Alex is away checking out sites for our new project, so I will be alone. Do you fancy coming with me?' she invited. I was taken aback. What was she after? Did she just want to crow over me and brag about her BAFTA win? I prevaricated, citing all manner of excuses not to go – then I thought why not? I hadn't got anything better to do, so I accepted.

Maggie

Did she say yes or no I wondered? It was difficult to tell after all the excuses for not coming she had dreamt up. I wish I hadn't asked her. What on earth are we going to talk about all week-end anyway? – If she is coming I can't think of one subject we would be able to discuss without a row ensuing. Try as we might, we still haven't bonded, even though we have both made an effort ever since Mum's illness knowing how much it means to her that we get on. I suppose I had better phone her to check if she is or isn't coming, and make arrangements where to meet -- if she is. I'm not going to let her get to me anymore. This is the happiest I have been in my entire life. I am married to a man I am deeply in love with, and he feels exactly the same way about me. Michael has progressed a lot since going to that amazing school, and even has a little job and he is thrilled about it. Career wise life couldn't be better. Apart for working with Alex's company, which is exciting, I am also being offered work in my own right, interviewing people for the networks, articles for the Nationals including the INFORMER, (Piers doesn't own it anymore) and next week I have been invited on the panel of Question Time. Not bad for the runt of the litter eh? Better phone my dear sister before I change my mind.

Helen

I'm not sure how I left it with Maggie? Did I make it clear I'd agreed to go with her. I'm really not sure. The phone is ringing, maybe that's her.

'Are you coming or not?' she asked in a tetchy voice.

'I said yes, didn't I?' I answered in a similar tone.

'Difficult to tell as you gave me so many reasons for not coming that I can't recollect whether you finally said yes or no' she countered. Not a great start to the week-end.

'We better meet at my house then.' she snapped giving me her address.

I asked Mum what her house was like. Very nice she replied. What sort of bland comment is that? Does she mean I don't like it, but don't want to say so? Or is she frightened of saying it was wonderful in case I become jealous? We'll soon find out I suppose.

Maggie had left the front door open, presumably for me, so I went inside and called out to her. 'Hi, come through to the back.' She shouted 'Sorry I'm not quite ready – make yourself at home.' I had to move piles of paper from the chair in order to sit down. Not quite sure where to put it I added it to one of the mountains of printed sheets on the floor It reminded me of Ruth's office when I first met her. What a tip: Mum wouldn't like this. They had some great political cartoons hung on the red walls which I reluctantly thought looked great.

'Sorry about that. The bloody phone never stops, and stupidly I can never ignore it. Let's get going.'

We drove down to Somerset in glorious sunshine. It had been ages since I had been anywhere outside of London and much to my surprise I found I was enjoying myself.

Maggie

I wish she would shut up about the loss of her bloody council seat for five minutes. I hope she is not going to keep it up the entire week-end.

'It gives you a wonderful feeling when you have been able to help one of your constituents.' she crowed. I bet the feeling is not altruism but power that she loves. Then she entered very dangerous territory with me by extolling the virtues of my bête noire, Margaret bloody Thatcher, so the first major row ensued before we were even half way to Somerset.

I think Helen thought I was about to turn round and drive back to London and she would miss out on a week-end in the country, so she backed down first. I was still steaming. Trying to placate me she changed the subject.

'Is it because we are doomed to be the opposite in everything we do or think as twins? According to Mum we are two magnetic halves of the same something or other that should join together and become one.' she quoted Mum, who was always telling us this.

'Perhaps we missed out on the magnets.' I said dismissively. 'We better keep off the politics for starters, and just accept there is not a single point we will be able to agree on that subject.'

As we neared the cottage the weather changed. We drove along in the gathering gloom, with the clouds becoming blacker and more threatening every minute. By the time we arrived, the rain was pounding the windows of the cottage with worrying strength and it had lost some of its charm, but Helen purred saying how pretty it was. Fortunately, I had stocked up with provisions before we left London, as I have never understood trading hours in rural areas.

That night the wind reached gale force and whistled round the chimney pots, making sleep impossible and there was an unsettling sound of tiles crashing and branches being ripped off the trees. The following morning the river had become a wild torrent and was lapping over the banks flooding part of the garden. Helen suggested maybe we should go home, but I was reluctant to leave the place unoccupied in case the house flooded, so we stayed. The area was prone to flooding, but Alex and I being dedicated townies, didn't think to check on a little thing like that when we put in an offer for the place. No wonder we got it at a bargain price.

Chapter forty-six
Helen 1990

We were both edgy: the wind does tend to cause unrest even in placid people, but neither of us could be described as that. Soon after we arrived the phone rang.

'That'll be Alex checking up on me.' Maggie said her eyes shining, and she took the call in another room. I could hear her laughing and murmuring, 'I love you too.' When she returned to the kitchen, a major row broke out between us but whatever triggered it became irrelevant when it turned venomous and personal. It was as if all my bottled up jealousy of her erupted and I remember screaming at her.

'You've always landed on your feet, lived in amazing homes and had money. You have no idea what it's like to be broke all the time and at the mercy of anyone who will give you a bed. How is it you managed to capture **two** successful handsome **SOLVENT** men, when you're not nearly as good looking as me?' I regretted saying that the minute the words left my mouth. It was puerile mentioning our looks.

'What have looks got to do with it?' she countered. I asked for that, but I just wanted to get one over on her.

'I slept with him you know.' That really was below the belt but I wanted to hurt her. 'Him? Who's 'the him' that you slept with?'

'Your precious Gerry.' Maggie looked stunned. 'When did you sleep with him? Not that I care,' she said defensively: he's history now.' but she looked upset never the less. She turned her back on me and started to unpack the food she had brought. This incensed me and I continued to belittle myself by letting out all the venom festering inside me because of her success. In retrospect I am ashamed of myself allowing her to make me lose my cool, but I was on fire now.

'I can write a thousand times better than you, but you're the one who has won prizes for stuff you have churned out, and all I have managed to do with my first class degree, is teach snotty nosed kids who don't want to know. Then she turned on me.

'Don't shove your bloody degree up my nose **again** please. Never a meeting between us or our Mother passes without both of you twittering on about it. Give it a rest for God's sake. Anyway, I have an Open University degree in English now. I didn't tell either you or Mum; because both of you would have belittled my success saying it was inferior to yours, and I wasn't going to give either of you the satisfaction of doing that.'

I really don't know what made me do what I did next. Years later I am still asking myself the same question. I grabbed a heavy skillet hanging on a butchers hook on one of those rack things that overhang a work surface in smart kitchens, and smashed her across her head with a force I didn't know I was capable of. I really don't know what made me do what I did next. Years later I am still asking myself the same question. I grabbed a heavy skillet hanging on a butchers hook on one of those rack things that overhang a work surface in smart kitchens, and smashed her across her head with a force I didn't know I was capable of. She crashed to the floor, and for one mini second, she looked at me in horror. I think I passed out at that point. When I came to I was dazed and confused and didn't know where I was.

It was pitch dark and the wind was howling around the chimney pots like a crowd of banshees. Still dazed, I idly wondered what the collective noun was for Banshees. Crowd didn't sound right. I put the light on and saw Maggie lying there and the full horror of what I had done came back to me. I had murdered my sister. I was shaking uncontrollably but had to pull myself together and think what to do to cover my crime. Her body --- I have to get rid of her body.

I stepped outside and noticed the river had risen to an alarming level and half of the garden was under water. That was the answer I thought -- the river. It was running so fast it will carry her downstream to wherever it ends up, and the bruise on her head could be explained by being hit by the amount of flotsam being carried along with the raging tide. I dragged her out of the cottage and down the muddy path to the water's edge and pushed her in.

Then-- as she hit the freezing water, she opened her eyes and shrieked; then made a brief attempt to swim before she was gathered up by the swirling waters, bouncing her on and off the banks as the river carried her down to the sea. Oh my God, she was still alive. I could have saved her; but I reacted too late. I was sobbing uncontrollably.

Pulling myself together I thought I might just get away with this if I just stay calm and think things through. Picking up one of the sandbags the volunteers had left for us yesterday, I placed it near the waters edge, hoping to make it appear that she had dropped it as she lost her footing and fell backwards into the river. I packed a few more of them around the kitchen doorway to make it look as if that was what she had in mind before she slipped and fell. Next I covered myself in mud to make it look as if I had slithered along on my stomach trying to save my sister. Damn, I should have pulled one of her shoes off to make it appear as if I had grabbed her ankles to save her from the water sweeping her away. Never mind. It's too late now. By a miracle the phone was still working so I dialled 999, sobbing as I did so, and reported the accident.

'Don't upset yourself,' a kindly voice at the end of the line told me. 'We'll be there in twenty minutes, maybe less.'

'Thank you. Please find my twin for me.'

'Twin eh? Be assured we will do everything we can to find her madam.'

I looked around to see what else I should do to back up my story. I cleaned up my vomit for starters. There was blood on the rush matting where I had dragged her body to the door. I wiped it over with a sponge to eliminate the stains then I heard a rescue boat chugging up the river. There was a policeman on board, who said he would stay behind to check out the area in and around the cottage.

'Give me the keys and I will return them to you at the rescue centre. Just routine he said smiling at me,' but I was worried and I began shaking.

'You're in shock love. Let's get you to the centre as quickly as possible and they will look after you.' the boatman told me as he wrapped a blanket round my shoulders. They took me to a school which was acting as an emergency centre, where people were arriving all the time, being rescued from the floods. It was all very efficient as they registered every new arrival and gave us all hot sweet tea which was apparently good for shock. Everybody thought I was sobbing for my lost twin, but it was ME I was crying for. How was I going to get away with this murder, because that is what I was. I had murdered my sister. How could I have done such a terrible thing?

A sympathetic policeman interviewed me, and I told him my trumped up story through my tears, and I'm pretty sure he believed me.

The following day the sun had the temerity to shine from an azure sky, and the wind had dropped, as if nothing had happened .I asked a policeman if he would phone her husband as I was too distressed to do so.

After signing my statement and filling in endless forms, I was allowed to return to London in Maggie's car. Driving home was a nightmare as the Somerset Levels were completely under water. It took hours. When I finally arrived in Fulham, coward that I am, I left the car outside their front door and fled. I wanted to build up my confidence a bit more before facing Alex. The police phoned me and told me her body had been washed up on the bank further downstream and that Alex was there to identify the body, so I was not required until the inquest.

Ten days later

The inquest: I was dreading it and naturally had to appear as a witness to what had happed. I sobbed all the way through it. Sophie was allowed to take me home and advised to give me a sedative to calm me down.

Later Alex phoned me to tell me the inquest had decided Maggie met her death by misadventure causing her to drown and had released her body for burial --- only she wasn't going to be buried, as she wanted to be cremated. He asked me again how the accident had happened, and could I have done anything to prevent it? I told him it happened the way I described at the inquest. I don't think he suspects anything; it's only my guilty conscience that makes me wonder if he doubts my involvement.

The day of the funeral arrived; I had been dreading it. Family and friends gathered together to mourn Maggie's passing, and judging by the numbers there, you would have thought it was royalty going to meet their maker, not some two bit journalist. What spell had she cast to attract so much adoration? Dad and Mum seemed shell shocked, which was only natural, Alex seemed to have shrunk, and all his vitality which was always evident with him, had vanished. Jennifer and Gerry – yes, he was there – were visibly distressed. But who on earth were all these other mourners? There are hundreds of them. I will have to put on a show to convince everyone that I loved her too. My children had refused to 'prop me up' as they put it, so I asked Rhys to escort me as it wouldn't do to go alone. I sobbed loudly learning on him, hopping my performance looked genuine.

'Why are you making such a drama? You never liked her.' he said, too loudly I thought. Did anyone hear him? I hope to God nobody did

Alex and Maggie had evidently made their wills and had discussed the type of funeral they would like -- not thinking they would need this information for thirty years or more. Maggie had requested a Humanist service as she *didn't believe all that God nonsense* which upset Mum. Alex said she had told him her love of animals didn't extend to feeding a load of bugs and their mates when she was in her cardboard box, so she wanted to be cremated. He tried to tell it like a joke, but his voice wavered and he looked so sad and defeated, it fell flat. He barely spoke to anyone, and was nowhere to be seen at the wake, which was not the jolly celebration of her life that Maggie had requested.

'Why can't she have a normal church funeral like everybody else?' I overheard Mum saying to Dad.

'Because she was different, although you could never see it.' Dad replied.

That surprised me. Was she his favourite? Alex was with his daughter Shirley from his first marriage, and she was crying as if Maggie had been her own mother. When I returned home, I found my kids had beaten me to it.

'Mum you were a total embarrassment at the funeral. You've always run her down, and would never let us contact her because you disliked her so much, so why were you weeping and wailing **so** loudly? Sophie admonished me. Ruth was giving me a sideways look.

'I agree, you did overdo it sweetie.' Ruth chipped in.

'How would you know? You weren't there?'

'Oh but I was'.

'Whatever for? You'd never even met her.'

'Curiosity darling—curiosity.'

I just wanted to get away from their accusing eyes, so I stomped of upstairs to my room.

Chapter forty-seven
Alex 1991

'I miss Maggie so much, I feel as if I can hardly breathe, or even want to anymore.. We had only been married briefly yet I cannot imagine a time when she wasn't my wife. The phone keeps ringing, with friends offering their sympathy and I just can't cope with answering the thing anymore. It's ringing now and the caller display said it was Jennifer and something told me to answer it this time. 'Do you want me to move out of the house?' I answered rather sharply. She sounded shocked.

'Alex whatever made you think that? I phoned to see how you were bearing up, and how Michael was dealing with the situation?'

'Oh, I am so so sorry Jennifer, I'm not thinking straight. That was unforgiveable of me to assume that was why you called, and extremely rude of me to speak to you as I did. Do forgive me. As for Michael, it's difficult to tell how he feels. Pat's with him at the moment. Do you want to speak to him?'

'Don't worry about it. I understand you're not yourself, and as its Maggie's house you are living in, you have every right to be there as her next of kin. It was given to her as part of her divorce settlement from my son Gerry, so it was hers to give and she would naturally leave it to you.. I am in London today. Can I call round?' she asked.

'Of course, I would be delighted to see you.' I told her sheepishly. I felt a real shit talking to her so harshly.

We sobbed and hugged each other telling each other stories of Maggie's life. Some made us laugh and others made us cry, but we both benefited from talking about her. I told of my concerns for Michael.

'It's so difficult to know what he is thinking. He doesn't talk about her so I don't know how to handle the situation .He can't comprehend why his mother isn't here and keeps asking where she is. Then out of the blue, he asked me 'Has she gone to heaven?' Where did he get that from? Pat and I said yes, not knowing what else to say.

'So we won't be seeing her again then?' he stated. It was if he had filed her away in a drawer, locked it, and that was it – Mummy didn't exist anymore. It upset me.

'That's the autism' Jennifer told me. 'Don't worry, he's not your problem he's my grandson. I will move to London for a while to take responsibility for him as I don't imagine Gerry will bother.'

'Move in here then, there's plenty of room as you know.' I told her. He may not be my son but I have grown fond of him since living with Mags.'

So she did, and as time passed Jennifer and I became good friends. Slowly, slowly, I threw myself into work and learnt to deal with my loss on a day to day basis. But I knew without a shadow of doubt that there would always be a void in my life that nobody other than Maggie could fill. I did eventually move out of the Fulham house as it was too painful to continue living there as I saw Maggie round every corner. Jennifer was adamant she should buy the house from me in spite of me telling her it wouldn't be necessary, but she insisted in paying me an over generous amount. I bought a flat nearby so I could continue to see Michael and her from time to time.

'Did Maggie ever finish her book on the Greenham women? Jennifer asked me one day when I had called round to see them.'

'I'm not sure how far she had got with it.' I replied.

'Why don't you complete it as a tribute to her?

That was a brilliant idea. I trawled through Maggie's computer, and downloaded the chapters and contacts she had listed, and went on from there. Feeling positive for the first time in months, I decided to make some calls tomorrow as she had listed all the interviews she had made. No I won't, I'll start right now.

Chapter forty-eight
Gerry & the Superintendent
1991

Gerry Macintyre had been selected to be the PPC (Prospective Political Candidate) for a ward in Somerset which by coincidence, was where Maggie's cottage was located.

When he applied to the selection board, nobody had told him about the number of Fund Raising functions, charity dinners and Bring and Buy Sales a PPC was expected to attend to get his name known throughout the constituency, and how often he had to put his hand in his pocket. He felt obliged to buy more raffle tickets than anyone else, BUT, even if he had the winning ticket it would have been frowned upon if he kept the prize. The incumbent MP for the area, George Reynolds, who was retiring at the next election, was supposed to introduce Gerry to the great and the good in his constituency, and in particular, those who would make generous donations to the party: but George was sulking. He didn't want the job any more, but was jealous of Gerry's early popularity, so didn't offer any help at all. Gerry's week-ends had become a drudge. He felt alone and unsupported and was beginning to regret putting himself forward as a candidate. His wife had informed him she wasn't standing for election, so why did she have to be bored out of her mind with all those Plebs? Plebs? He realised early in their relationship that The Honourable Jane was not a great supporter of democracy, but dedicated member of the self-preservation party. The selection committee were not best pleased at her absence, as they expected the wife of their chosen one to do her bit at fund raising events, and as Gerry's wife was an honourable, they felt this would go down rather well with the snobbier members of the electorate when she handed them a cup of tea at a function. They were to be disappointed.

Gerry was doing his bit building up his local profile there one week-end when he found himself sitting next to Superintendent Mike Seymour at a fund raising dinner which he had been given to understand was for the Save the Whales campaign. Wrong! His prepared speech was rendered useless as he discovered the money was destined for a deprived school somewhere in Africa. Panic set in and he had to make discreet enquiries ASAP to find out more about the charity's aims, and in which country in that vast continent the school was located, then rewrite his speech in his head. No time to commit it to paper.

Gerry had written to the Chief Constable requesting a meeting, but feeling a bit miffed, found himself palmed off with a Superintendent. After making some obligatory small talk with him, he expressed some of the concerns he had about Maggie's death.

'My ex-wife was drowned in the floods around here,' he reminded the Mike, 'and I have felt uneasy about the findings of the enquiry ever since.'

'Why's that sir?'

'Well she was staying in her cottage with her sister at the time ...

'Oh yes I remember. Twins weren't they; I understand they were very close?'

'On the contrary, they hated each other, and I am mystified as to why they were even together in Maggie's cottage.'

'The findings of the enquiry misadventure causing death by drowning if I recall. It seemed quite clear cut and were not questioned at the inquest Sir, so may I ask why you are troubled by the result?'

'Oh please call me Gerry. I attended her funeral, and couldn't believe the performance Helen, her sister, put on with her loud sobbing. It struck me as totally false, because as far as I know they hadn't spoken for years. They never had any communication with each other all the time we were together. Maybe Helen knows something about the so called accident the rest of us don't?'

'That is very interesting Sir - sorry Gerry, I will look into it and be in touch.'

Gerry thanked him and changed the subject and asking the sort of questions PPCs usually ask high ranking police officers, subjects like crime rates in the area, was there a drug problem etc. He then nervously delivered his unprepared speech to the audience. It was disappointingly brief the charity's supporters felt.

Mike Seymour was very keen on being the first to introduce any new detection methods in his constabulary the minute they were available. He was an avid reader of science reports and magazines so as not to miss anything that could help the police clear up rates, and he was very excited about the research going on in Cambridge University at the moment' about something called Deoxyribonucleic Acid (DNA) which sounded ground breaking for future detection work.

He was not happy attending these Fund Raising events. A waste of police time he thought kowtowing to local so called dignitaries, -- not his style at all, he complained: but neither was it the Chief Constable nor his deputy – and definitely not Mike's Line Manager, Chief Superintendent Miles Grayston. He hated politicians whatever their political persuasion with a passion, and avoided them at all costs, so Mike; not for the first time, found himself having been passed down the line to ingratiate with the dedicated charity volunteers touting their begging bowls; all in the line of duty. Gerry may not be elected yet, but it was highly likely he would be at the next General Election and he seemed a nice chap, so Mike decided to re-examine the case himself.

He was curious about Gerry's comments on the animosity between the Sutherland twins, and decided to inspect Maggie's cottage himself to see if anything had been missed. He grabbed a hapless young PC Ray Walker to accompany him.

'Get me a copy of the accident report' he barked. Quaking, Ray scuttled off in search of the file. Mike, at six foot three and with a rugby player's physic and deep booming voice was an intimidating figure and he used it to his advantage when he felt the occasion warranted it. He would loom over suspects staring them straight in the eye, often eliciting an early confession of guilt from them. Unfortunately he was known to have the same effect on some of the coppers in his station, who also quaked in his presence. Ray Walker was one of those affected.

'Had the kitchen been checked for prints?' he barked.

'Don't think so Sir 'cos they were twins, so the prints would be the same wouldn't they?' he replied smugly.

'Which idiot decided that? It's the **only** way you can tell identical twins apart is by their finger prints.'

'Dunno Sir' DC Walker replied looking decidedly sheepish. The Chief sighed. The cottage was in a remote area so it was unlikely anyone had been there in the intervening months so he looked at the footprints still imprinted in the dried mud. He was suspicious, something wasn't quite right, and what was that solitary sandbag doing there? Odd! He examined the skid marks which also looked unnatural. Going into the cottage he noticed a skillet on the work surface that wasn't even mentioned in the original report. Had that been checked thoroughly for prints? Probably not, but as it had a wooden handle it was possible there were still detectable prints on it - **if** it hadn't been handled since the accident that is. He knew Alex had left the cottage after the inquest without even looking inside so there was a good chance of finding prints.

It rather looked to Mike, that whatever the sister had told the investigating officer he had believed without question he thought. A pretty girl I expect. How many pretty girls got away with murder, because some DC imagined what it would be like getting into her knickers? Quite a few I'm sure, he thought, remembering when he was a young PC.

'Bag that skillet up Walker. – NO you fool, don't put your dabs all over it. There's a carrier bag on that chair, use that. Put your hand inside the bag before you pick it up so you don't transfer your prints onto the handle.' PC Walker thought the chief was the fool, not him. It was obvious to him this case had been an accident. Then Mike spotted a dark patch on the wooden step leading out of the house. Could that be blood? Was she killed in the kitchen then dragged down to the river the chief pondered?

'Get SOCO (Scene of Crime officers) down here. I want the place going over again.' he ordered PC Walker, I want the area retested for finger prints and blood deposits: then double check the door step and the kitchen floor under the rush mat for traces of blood.' That seems to have been missed at the original investigation. It looks clean enough on the surface, but blood would have seeped through the rushes he told them and he was subsequently proved right

In her haste to clean the floor covering before the rescue boat arrived, Helen hadn't paid any attention to the skillet. Silly girl, that was the murder weapon, and it turned out to be her downfall. Finger and blood traces on the pan were confirmed as Helen's but with their blood type being identical as they were twins would not be conclusive proof. It had been noticed at the initial investigation, that Helen had a small scar on her right forefinger from a long forgotten accident, but it made it possible to identify the prints on the skillet handle as hers. The dark stain on the doorstep proved to be blood just as Mike thought.

The photographs of the severe bruising on Maggie's head were re-examined in the light of this new evidence and were found to be anti- mortem, but all the other wounds on her body were post mortem, obtained when she was swept downstream in the flood. Blood was identified in the rush matting covering the floor and traces were found on the wooden step. Mike was feeling smug.

'Aren't I always telling you the importance of checking EVERY surface, every corner, and every blade of grass at the scene? The evidence we are now confronted with was all there day one of this case, and was missed through lack of attention to DETAIL. Let this be a lesson to you all. Dismiss.' Duly chastened, they moved off to their various departments. A murder enquiry was opened.

'The evidence is going to be difficult to prove without the body so we need to get a confession from Mrs Capstic he told DI Browning, otherwise we won't get a conviction. The DI had originally thought the Superintendent had lost it digging up this case. The victim – if she was a victim – had been cremated so could not be re-examined he said to anyone who would listen. He was not quite so cocky when the lab reports turned up. The way things are turning out, maybe I should take more notice of some of his chief's ideas.

'I will sit in when you interview her 'the Superintendent informed him.

'Certainly Sir. I will send a couple of the men up to London to arrest her'

'Not yet, the evidence is only circumstantial. Just bring her in for further questioning, but bring her here never the less.'

Chapter forty-nine
Helen April 1991
Six months after Maggie's death

The kids in my class have been very gentle with me since I returned to work Maybe I have misjudged them. Maggie had taken me to task over this. Oh why am I thinking about her? I just want to forget she ever existed. Sometimes I find myself shaking when I remember what happened and I had to seek help from a doctor, who gave me a sedative which makes me feel woozy.

I think Ruth has an idea that there is something I'm not telling her. She hasn't said anything, but her demeanour gives that impression. A strange friendship has developed between her and Richard. He has a job, if you can call it that, shelf stacking in a super market at night. But I suppose ex-cons are not employer's first choice to recruit as a members of staff, so maybe, be it ever so humble, he's lucky to have a job at all. He tells me he will need a reference saying how reliable he is for his next job which will hopefully be higher up the social scale. He is very distant with me when he comes to see the kids, and then he scuttles down to see Ruth. Sometimes my kids go to the cinema with them, and I'm left in the house on my own. It's all very odd. Sophie tells me she thinks Ruth and her father are thinking of opening a restaurant together. He was very cagey when I asked him if this was true.

I'm feeling very lonely at the moment and seem to be in a state of limbo. .A boyfriend would help the situation, but I'm forty four now so I don't get the pick of the bunch. The choice seems limited to married men wanting a non-committal affair, divorced men moaning about their ex's huge alimony pay outs, or guys checking out what their sexual preference is.

I called on Mum and Dad today. They are devastated over Maggie's death, and Mum keeps weeping and wailing over how badly she treated her when she was alive.

'I never understood her.' she sobbed. Dad piped up.

'You didn't try. You wanted the girls to be exactly the same because they were twins when they were two completely different people, Isn't that right Helen?' Dad was obviously looking for an ally, as I think Mum was getting on his nerves.

'Probably Dad, -- I don't know. Sorry, I'm off now, things to do – 'love you both' and fled. I couldn't stand the atmosphere any longer.

Then my world, dull as it was, fell apart. There was a banging on the door along with the persistent ringing of the bell

'Alright, alright, I'm coming. Stop making that racket 'I shouted opening the door. There were two burley policemen there on the door step.

'What on earth do you want that necessitates making such a row,' I challenged them

'Are you Helen Sutherland Capstic? The taller one asked. Fear engulfed me. Ruth had come half way down the stairs, wondering what all the noise was about.

'We need you to give us your statement again to the events on the night of the 1 October 4th 1990, and the death of Mrs Margaret Sutherland

McDonald, also to check your finger prints in the light of new evidence. Its only routine ma'am but we need you to accompany us back to Somerset. Nothing to worry about.'

'I must have repeated my statement at least six times already, and why do you want my fingerprints again?' I questioned them looking at them straight in the eyes but quaking inside. What evidence could they have found?

'Are you prepared to accompany us voluntarily ma'am or would you prefer me to arrest you?' He said this in a friendly gentle voice defying the seriousness of his request.

'Arrest me?' I yelled at him 'What for. My sister's death was an accident. I insisted. 'There was an inquest and I was exonerated.' By this time my daughter and my son, joined Ruth on the stairs to witness my humiliation. As I left with the police. I heard Ruth ask, 'Shouldn't one of us have gone with her?' but I was whisked off before anyone offered.

Arriving at the police station, I was greeted by Superintendent Mike Seymour who was charming, so I smiled at him sweetly.

'Follow me to the interview room' Mrs Capstic.

'I use my birth name Sutherland now, and perhaps you will at least allow me to visit the bathroom before you interrogate me?'

'Apologies ma'am of course.'

When I returned from the loo I was surprised to see that he and a DI were going to be the ones to interview me.

Chapter fifty
Mike Seymour and the DI

'As I said before, without a body we are going to have to push Mrs Capstic hard for a confession, Mike said to DI Brian Browning, 'some of our evidence is circumstantial, and it may be hard to prove she did it with what we've got. I'm going to lead the interview. You don't mind do you Brian?'

The station boss, DI Brian Browning did mind, he minded very much and was furious. It was a terrible imposition of the Super he felt. Did Mike doubt his ability to question the culprit?'

'No problem Sir. Be my guest,' what else could he say?' He hadn't met Mike Seymour before he was the Superintendent, so he wasn't aware of his reputation as an interrogator.

'Make yourself comfortable Mrs Capstic ...'

'I did tell you, I have reverted to my single name now.' she replied coyly.

'My apologies Ms Sutherland. Why did you kill your sister on the night of 14th October 1990' Mike Seymour asked.

'What do you mean? I didn't kill my sister,' she said with panic in her voice.

'Oh forgive me I thought you did.

DI Browning couldn't believe what he had just heard the Super say. He had no right to speak to the suspect in that manner, whatever he might think. He would have severely reprimand, -- even demoted him, if he had accused her in such a way.

'I need to turn the recorder on Sir, and caution Mrs Sutherland.'

'Of course Brian; very remiss of me. Apologies.'

The bastard knew the recorder wasn't switched on Brian thought. He was trying to unnerve the poor woman.

The interrogation followed along conventional lines after that, much to Brian's relief.

'How did Mrs McDonald get that bruise on the side of her head? Who else was in the cottage? Mike questioned.

'Nobody, she probably got that when she was in the river being bounced against the bank'

'Oh silly me, that's what you said at the inquest wasn't it. Then what was that skillet on the worktop with both yours and your sisters blood on it used for? Frying eggs?' He hoped she didn't realise their blood group would be the same.

'I can't image how they got there,' she spluttered.

'I understand from someone close to your family that you were sworn enemies. May I suggest you had a row that got out of hand and you grabbed the nearest weapon you could lay your hands on and smashed Mrs McDonald on the side of her head with a ferocious whack?'

'No, no, no, who from my family would say such a thing.' she sobbed. I loved my sister.

'I don't think so Ms Sutherland.'

''She was patronising me and . . .'

'Patronising you? Eh! She was a very successful woman wasn't she? You must have felt undermined by her and understandably jealous of her success and felt justified in getting your own back on her. Is that right?' he positively purred as he said this lulling Helen into a false sense of security.

'Yes she ... No, no I didn't,' Helen was sobbing loudly by now, knowing Mike had got her. I didn't mean to kill her' she sobbed.

'Helen Sutherland -- Capstic, I am arresting you for the murder .....' 'What are you talking about? That's nonsense; she was, drowned in an accident.'

'... of Margaret Sutherland McDonald. You do not have to say anything ....'

'I didn't murder her she slipped...'

'But, it may harm your defence if you do not mention ...'

'You are making a very big mistake . . .'

'...when questioned something you later rely on in court ...'

'My brother in law is an MP. He will speak to your ...'

'Superior the word you are looking for ma'am,' Mike interrupted. Gerry Macintyr is NOT an MP yet and it was he who alerted me to his concerns about the results of the inquest, I don't think calling him will help your case, do you?

He continued, '...anything you do say may be given in evidence.

She burst into tears. 'It was an accident. I didn't mean to kill her. She fell backwards picking up that sandbag.'

Got her, he thought. 'I could never be able to charge her on the flimsy evidence we had, 'You didn't mean to kill her eh? Shall I take that as a confession ma'am?

'No no no. You made me nervous and I made a mistake. It was an accident as I said before.'

He had tricked her into confessing, but now she had retracted her remark.

'I don't think so ma'am. We have presented irrefutable evidence to the contrary. Take her down.'

Her solicitor insisted it should go to trial.

At the trial Mike left it to his DI to give the police evidence against Helen.

'The DI was still smarting that he hadn't lead the investigation, and now the bastard was leaving it to him to face the barrister's inquisition.

'Yes, you're right Sir. I will do my best Sir even though I **didn't** actually conduct the interview with Ms Sutherland Capstic, and will hopefully remember the questions you asked.' Mike scowled at him, was Brian being sarcastic?

At the trial Helen's barrister tried to cast doubt as to which twin's prints were on the handle of the skillet as their blood type was identical because they were twins,

The Crown Prosecution barrister pointed out that twin's blood type may be identical, but their fingerprints were not. He then gave a comical physical demonstration of the impossibility of Maggie smashing the skillet over her own head, causing unbridled mirth in the court and demolishing the defence's argument. She was convicted of manslaughter and sent to prison for ten years.

'You've made a mistake she told the jury, I loved my sister I didn't mean to kill her.' As she delivered her plea, she turned her beautiful blue eyes towards them, making the men wonder if she was innocent after all.

"She's a manipulator isn't she?" one of the women jurors whispered to her colleague. "Yeah, we know her type don't we? We were right to convict her 'cos she's as guilty as hell" she replied.

Epilogue
Helen 1995

After serving five years of my sentence, I was released from prison early for good behaviour. My daughter Sophie picked me up outside the gates heavily disguised with huge dark glasses, a big floppy hat, and an expression of total disgust on her face. I recalled the time I met Richard from prison also heavily disguised, after his brush with the law, so I did understand just how embarrassed she felt being associated with a criminal. She didn't take me home to Ruth's place as I had hoped (not that I had heard a word from her for five years) but to a tiny flat at the scruffy end of Notting Hill, where she dumped me giving me instructions of where the dustbin was located; where I should pay my rent and precious little else. I almost wished I was back in prison. At least I had friends there, and an odd sort of social life.

For the first six months of my incarceration I tried to keep a very low profile -- not wanting to mix with what I thought then 'were these dreadful ignorant women'. Now I am deeply ashamed of myself to have even thought that, let alone said it. They used to call me the duchess in a very sneering way goading me all the time and would do things like jogging my elbow, so my food tray would crash to the floor. Then I would be ordered by the screws to clean it up, which would be greeted with whoops of glee. I hated them with a passion then. In retrospect, why did I always have such a high opinion of myself, because I really hadn't achieved a great deal in my life. It pains me to say it, but Maggie was the achiever, not me.

I had to see the prison psychologist every week for a while. He kept asking me 'did I regret killing my sister?' What sort of daft question was that? Of course I regretted it. I didn't mean to kill Maggie but I did, and I paid the price for my crime. I saw no point in dwelling on what happened as I couldn't change anything or bring her back to life. He must have thought I was a cold calculating bitch as he didn't bother with me after that session.

Loneliness eventually drove me to climb down off my high horse. I felt so isolated I needed to talk to someone – anyone, but it was difficult at first as nobody wanted to talk to me. Not surprising really seeing I'd snubbed them for months: also they didn't trust me because of what they thought was my 'posh accent'. I was accused of being the 'guv'nor's spy. Subsequently I did make some friends, genuine ones, rather than the false ones I had on the outsider.

I discovered that it was not always the women's fault they had ended up in prison. Many of them were single parents who had fallen into prostitution and crime to make ends meet. Drug addiction was a major problem amongst them too. The dealers method was to get these venerable women hooked on drugs then used them as expendable deliverers of their poison. Inevitably many of them ended up in prison. A high proportion of the women had suffered domestic violence from brutal husbands. I remember when Maggie wrote an article about it, and Mum and I thought it was grossly exaggerated. Well it wasn't; she was right and we were wrong.

I was 'persuaded' by the prison governor, to work with the Shannon Trust (a charity for women prisoners) by teaching some of the women to read. Their inability to do so had often been the cause of many of their problems.

'Don't get on the wrong side of her. She can make life hell for you' Trudy, one of my new friends advised me. Back then I believed that anyone leaving school without the basic skills meant they were lazy, thick, or just plain bolshie. I remember Maggie taking me to task over this when we were travelling down to the cottage. I wasn't very nice to my pupils when I started teaching them, but then it started to dawn on me that I had misjudged these women and there were many factors that contributed to their ignorance that were not always of their own making. Disrupted schooling when families were on the move from one unsuitable home to another: single parents unable to cope, who kept their older children at home to help look after the younger ones, ineffectual teachers who couldn't keep control of classes that were far too big. Was I one of those? The list was endless.

I found it difficult adjusting to life outside the prison gates at first. I changed my name and now call myself Helen Rushton, which was Mum's maiden name. Capstic was an unusual enough name to jog memories of Richard – another ex-prisoner in the family. Sophie visited me occasionally when I was incarcerated but she barely spoke to me and it was exactly the same when she called at the flat. I would like to have had some news of the family but no such luck: I only received monosyllabic grunts from my disapproving daughter.

By chance I ran into Trudy Metcalf in Oxford Street. I was thrilled as I wanted to get in touch with her, but I had no way of doing so. Oh joy, it turned out she only lived a couple of tube stops away from my flat. Meeting her again has given some meaning to my life. She was released a couple of years ago, and was helped by an ex-prisoners charity to adjust to life outside of prison. Now she works for them as a paid employee: a brilliant turnaround from her life of petty crime.

'Come and work for us' she said, 'you could help by teaching some of the ex con's to read, like you did inside. More importantly, you could help them to fill in the endless forms they get but don't understand, so they can get some money to live on.

Have you managed to find a job?' Not waiting for me to respond she continued. 'No 'course you 'aven't. Nobody wants us, particularly in respectable jobs like yours. Do you want to spend the rest of your life feeling sorry for yourself? I bet you don't.'

She was right. I had fallen into the trap of not going out and watching daytime television, which bored me to death, so I decided to join her at the charity, which was one of the best decisions I made in my life.

Sophie's attitude to me softened after I starting working there. 'Maggie would be pleased' she said. I wasn't sure how to react to that. . She told me she was working part time with Richard and Ruth in their restaurant while she was studying. *Their restaurant*? What restaurant? How did they even know each other?' I quizzed her.

'Oh Dad has lived at Ruth's ever since you went to prison' she said casually 'The restaurant's a great success. The customers choose their cut of meat then cook it at their table, a fantastic idea don't you think?'

'Yes.' I replied feebly. When Ruth ran the idea past me years ago I thought was just another one of her crackpot ideas and it would never take off. Ah well; wrong again! I thought I would leave my questions for another time. 'Don't want to upset my daughter so early in our new relationship.

Eventually I learned Richard had reined in Ruth's crazy spending habits from the outset of their joint venture. It was her inability to keep control of the finances that had led. to the demise of *THE GO GETTER.*

Her original idea for the restaurant was for customers to bring in their own meat to cook. He stopped that straight away. Firstly where was the profit in that? Secondly the health authorities would be down on them as there would be no control of the origins or quality of the meat coming into the restaurant.

As Ruth's wealthy father saw how well his beloved daughter was doing with Richard in charge of the finances, he invested some of his money into the venture which meant they could spend more on the decor, making it modern and inviting.

'I've got an idea he thought that would bring the two of them closer together, and she might give up being a lesbian and marry Dad.' Sophie laughed.

'He'll be lucky, poor man.' Had she guessed about Ruth's and my relationship? Oh God, I hope not. I found myself blushing.

'The restaurant's fab' she enthused. Fab? What sort of word is that I thought, but said nothing?

Sophie persuaded Mum to come and see me at my new flat. It was a tearful meeting with recriminations on both sides, but it lifted a heavy burden from me as I missed my mother.

I don't think Dad will ever forgive me though, as it appears mum went into some sort of coma for months after I was found guilty, and it was thought she may never recover. He's always adored Mumso I can't blame him for not wanting to see me.

Sophie told me Jason (my son) was a solicitor and was married with two small children. I'm a grandmother. How exciting, but I doubt if I will ever be allowed to meet them.

'I don't see them very often as I don't get on with Charlotte'. I presumed Charlotte was his wife but I didn't like to ask in case she bit my head off, as she was wont to do at times. A big disappointment to me was that Sophie had dropped out of university, where she was studying law. She decided she didn't enjoy the course and wanted to be a journalist, and had turned to Alex for help. I was amazed that he would have anything to do with any daughter of mine – the killer of his beloved Maggie.

'Whatever did he say when you went to see him?' I asked her.

'He had just won a literary prize as he had completed a book Maggie had started about the Greenham Common women and was interviewed on TV so I used that as an 'intro by saying I had seen him and congratulated him on his achievement. He looked a bit shattered when he first realised who I was, but then said it wasn't my fault my mother was a jealous evil murdering witch, but as I was Maggie's niece, he would naturally help.' she said quite casually. Furious, I opened my mouth to counter his remark, but I bit my tongue, just saying that it was kind of him to help her.

'Do you want to meet him? She asked unexpectedly. I shuddered and went cold all over. 'No –No I couldn't face him.' I stuttered. 'Whatever made you suggest such a thing?' I had only spoken to Alex briefly after the 'accident' and not at all since my arrest. He probably wouldn't want to see me anyway, and I am not brave enough to face him, so I hope Sophie won't progress this daft idea, but I had a sneaking feeling she might.

I've been punished for my crime by being imprisoned, but much as I am enjoying my work with the ex-prisoners, I do feel my life is in some sort of limbo and I need to move on and will only be able to do that when I have resolved the past. Meeting up with Alex and my Dad might allow me to apologise for the grief I caused them and give me some sort of closure even if they don't accept my contrition. Shall I write before meeting them? What on earth can I say? Do I want to meet them? Not really but I feel that it's probably what I need to do. No, perhaps I should let sleeping dogs lie as the cliché goes. Maybe it's too soon? No it's not; I'm just prevaricating and avoiding facing my demons. I'll speak to Sophie to see what she thinks.

Printed in Poland
by Amazon Fulfillment
Poland Sp. z o.o., Wrocław